The Magwitch Legacy

The Magwitch Legacy

Tony Lester

Introduction

When Abel Magwitch was transported, along with Compeyson, to Australia, he was helped there by a previously transported woman. This was Amanda Jane who eventually became Lady Spens. Magwitch's protégé, Pip Pirrip came to Australia when Magwitch died. At first, he was befriended by Lady Spens, then, he went to the goldfields where he met John Adam. He went into business with John Adam, disappointing Estella who also came to Australia looking for him.

Lady Spens had a maid who was also a convict who had been transported. She married an ex soldier, and together they set up a bookshop in Sydney and had two children. Their daughter, Olivia, married Phillip Gargery who was a blacksmith and came to New South Wales looking to make a better life there away from what he saw as a corrupt and oppressive England.

Now in 1891, Olivia and her husband and their young son, Arthur, known to all as Art, seem to be moving towards a more peaceful time, having endured an unsettled period where Phillip's drinking caused problems. They have a bookshop and Phillip is trying to behave in a more mature fashion.

The Magwitch Legacy

Livvy's Story

Chapter 1

When my mother died my father came back from the dead to help her into the next world. I was told this was so by the black woman who cared for her in the last days of her life. That woman was to cause me much trouble. I had already found out from Mrs Kaye, her employer how, my mother had been of great help to Mrs Kaye. I was not surprised to hear this. My mother's life was that of a transported convict to New South Wales which was ever marked by her willingness to help others. She could have been bitter; she had every right to be, but she turned her face from such an attitude and instead concentrated upon being positive. Indeed, at times she went much further to aid those who she thought less fortunate than she.

In England she was bullied because she had a lop-sided face, and eventually appeared to go mad and attacked Jem Akenhead, a footmen in the house where she was a maid. She had already lost her mother; she never ever talked about her father who I expect deserted her mother when he saw that he had a disfigured daughter.

My mother had contracted small-pox and that made her features worse. With such a poor start to life you might have thought that when she appeared at court for the attack that they could have been merciful. They weren't. I remember her telling me that the judge told her that that she, Jane Alambard, was a wicked depraved creature who had set myself up against a good God who had seen fit to make sure that, through giving her a distorted face, she was fit to serve with the lowest part of society. He told her that he would normally have sentenced her to hang, but he wanted to give her a chance to her, so ordered her to be transported for life to New South Wales.

Possibly it was the best thing that could have happened to her, for in Australia she was employed by someone who treated her with the sort of kindness that she had never experienced up to then.

She married my father, who was a soldier serving in Australia, and together they ran a successful bookshop until it was burned down, and mysteriously my father died. But why am I telling you all this? Her story and the story of that part of my life has been told elsewhere. Now I want to tell you how Phillip Gargery and I made our way through life with Arthur Phillip John Gargery our son.

Our lives changed completely when we discovered the gold that Pip Pirrip had unwittingly given us. At that time we had lost our shop and had been cheated by Toby. We were only just managing to get by.

Now with what we got for the gold I was able to make sure that my ma was well cared for, despite the fact she was surrounded by blacks, and we were able to buy a small shop with premises above it, and rooms to the back. Phillip or Pip, as I always called him was a changed man. He gave up the drink and the boxing. Toby's death had shaken him. Naturally in his time he seen similar violent deaths, but this was one in which he was involved. Coupled with that was the way that we came together to face our problems as a proper married couple.

Here I must be completely honest. Up to this time I had been cold towards my husband. If I examine my behaviour it becomes clear to me that I was influenced by a number of things. The first of these was the way in which I let Estella dictate my behaviour. I thought that she was exactly how I should be. It was years before I came to realise that despite her strength of character she had flaws.

Yes, she was a determined able woman, determined to overcome the dreadful business of finding out the shocking fact that her mother was a murderer. Her refusal to deny her past and to accept it boldly fed into my attitude where I clung to the fact that my mother was a transported convict. Now I began to see that although I was right not to be ashamed that I was a convict's daughter, I was wrong to continue to glory in it.

I realise too now that my stubborn refusal to grow up and be myself, and not a stupid little girl, made matters worse between Pip and me. I blamed him all the time. He did drink to excess, but I never asked why he behaved as he did. Of course my Ma had been transported in a convict ship; of course she been made practically a slave when she was rescued from the Parramatta women's factory; and of course when she married a common soldier she remained in most people's eyes no more than a lucky ex-convict. I let that get in the way of seeing my husband for what he really was.

He was just an honest blacksmith. He was just what you might expect a blacksmith to resemble; well-built with muscles developed by his work and large rough hands. Only his face might give you pause, and might make you ask questions, for no blacksmith normally got such a battered visage from his work. So where did it come from? It came from boxing. I only saw him in the ring on one occasion and I never wanted to see it again. How can they call it a sport? Before I turned away I remember being amazed though at how, big man that he was, he skipped so lightly around that ring.

I suppose that the main thing that made Pip change (by the way, some called him Pip just as I did) was the birth of Arthur Phillip John, our son who eventually was called Art by everyone. He was our one child. I came to childbirth late in life; I was thirty-eight, and we had no more. I really believe Pip knew that he had to settle down at last when he eventually held his son in his arms. The other thing that steadied him was the amount of employment that came his way as a result of knowing James Barnet. After a spell of employment, Pip was left high and dry so I cajoled him into seeking out James Barnet. He didn't want to. He could be so stubborn at times!

Now they say that leopards don't change their spots and that you can't teach an old dog new tricks. These are just the kind of sayings that my mother used to utter. She always said as how she heard them from her mother. I wondered at times how she could have heard them all for she also said that she was not long with her mother before she went into service. Well, she's gone now, so I shall never get the chance to quiz her. But my Pip Gargery was living proof that these two adages could be proved wrong. For not only did he stop his wild drinking and fighting, but he also changed from a skilled blacksmith to skilled electrician, so there!

Now I must not boast, but I have to own that I was the one who brought about the latter change. It all started before

Pip had to run off.   It was all on account of the fact that I was an avid reader and that I found out Pip's amazing ability to memorize everything he read so that he was able to repeat it word for word immediately afterwards! I found this out at that time when James Barnet's Garden Palace was to be constructed in the Botanical Gardens in Sydney. I read in a newspaper that the palace had to be finished in time for the 1879 Sydney International Exhibition so they were going to use electric light. My plan was for him to learn something about electricity so that he could steal a march on the other workers.I accordingly urged him to use this skill of instant memory recall to good effect. Well, he did so, and he got taken on and would have gradually become more successful except for that trouble about a fight that meant him having to run off into the bush.

When he came back it was just in time to rescue me from Toby, but that's all done with now. Like I said, I persuaded him to seek out James Barnet and sure enough he was soon in employment once again.

One day he came home to say that there was an opening for some one with knowledge of electricity. I cross-examined him about what the requirements were. He recited them to me from memory having read the details on a specification sheet. A few days later I told him that he ought to apply.

"You can do that."

"I don't know enough. They will require more."

"So learn more!"

"How do I do that?"

I pushed more books towards him that I had put aside when he had first got involved in this work back in 1878.

"I know that you don't always understand what you read, so read it and ask what it means."

"But who shall I ask?"

Mr Butler, Mr Leonard Butler. I have spoken with him and he is agreeable that he should assist you in this endeavour.

Unbeknownst to Pip I had left young Art with a good friend of ours, Elizabeth Wright, called Liz by everyone. She absolutely doted upon our child, having none of her own. I then went to see Leonard Butler, a skilled craftsman who had been in the electrical business until that nasty accident, after which he worked no more. I had known him for some time for he was an avid reader and a frequent caller at our shop.

"Leonard. We both know that you have considerable experience in this electricity business, and sadly, you are now no longer able to seek employment."

"That is correct. You have, as usual hit the proverbial nail right upon the proverbial head. Which, as I have so frequently said, is so typical of you."

He was about to add more, but I stopped him with a question.

"Would I be asking too much of our friendship to do me, and Pip, of course, the greatest of favours?"

Leonard cocked his head sideways and fixed an old eye upon me. He said nothing, but waited. He may run on a bit, but he also knows when to be silent.

"He needs instruction in that calling and craft where you once were so eminent, so that he can enter employment on much more favourable terms that he receives at present."

"Aha!"

"I shall, of course, offer you a suitable reimbursement."

He held up his hand, exhibiting to my horror the frightful effect that his dreadful fall and the fire had had upon it. Seeing my look, he hastily withdrew the limb, covering it with his shirtsleeve.

"My dear Liv, I hope that our long acquaintance, nay, our long friendship allows me to presume to call you in such terms, I should be honoured and deem it a pleasure to be able to transmit what small stock of knowledge I have to your husband. He is off the drink permanently?" he added anxiously.

"Absolutely!"

"Splendid!"

He relaxed and sat back and said:

"You know better than anyone, my dear, the state to which I am brought to, so I know that you will forgive my asking about the precise terms of the remuneration."

"As to that I can only offer a small fee", but as his face fell, I added quickly:

"You can however, have the small room at the back of the shop, where you shall be snug and as well fed as any in this household, for we shall all eat together. No rum, of course, but enough beer to keep you healthy."

After some delicate verbal to-ing and fro-ing, which we both enjoyed, the terms were agreed by us both.

Chapter 2

My foray into the world of work for men had made me aware that women were in no fashion given anything like the rights of men. And, similarly, they had limited voting rights. This made me interested in women's rights generally. I had already followed in the newspapers how the Victorian Women's Suffrage Society had been formed in Victoria in 1884, so when the Australian Women's Suffrage Society was formed in 1889 I mentioned as casually as possible to Pip that I would like to join it. His response was not enthusiastic. He wanted change, but not the kind that might be brought about by women.

He wanted to know whether I had enough time for such nonsense. Did I not have my hands full with a child to rear and a shop to run, not to mention a home and a husband to care for? I had heard Maybanke Wolstenholme speak on more than one occasion however, and I knew that I could bring Pip round to my way of thinking. I would marshal the arguments that I had heard her espouse and use them. And, of course, now that I had organised help for him he could hardly refuse my simple request. In the face of my gentle feminine verbal onslaught, along with a few special meals, he softened. I went down to the Australian Women's Suffrage Society while he was still in a good mood and joined.

The Australian Women's Suffrage Society had been formed in 1889, and I knew, because I had read all about it in the newspapers, that they aimed to educate women and men about a woman's right to vote. They also wanted everyone to know that women had a right to stand for parliament. Not a right in law that is, but a right that came with the acceptance that men and women were equal. When I said this to Lizbeth she replied that everyone knew that men were different to women, so they couldn't be equal, so there!

When I was passed over for nurse training it had upset me. Lizbeth's advice on that occasion was to accept my fate. I had done. Now I was changed. I was better at standing up for myself, so why should I not stand up for my rights?

Oh dear! What had I done? Surrounded by the sort of 'good women' who had been the model for Mrs Jellyby, a philanthropist in Dicken's 'Bleak House', I felt at times that I could scream with frustration. How they talked! It was always talk. In the end I sought out Maybanke Wolstenholme and said how disappointed I was.

She looked at me. She had come as an immigrant from Kingston upon Thames in England and I thought that she would understand my frustration, as it was well known that she had suffered from a husband who drank to excess. He had left her to fend for herself and her answer was to start a school for women. I thought that she would be sure to come out with some grand idea that enabled me to leap into action.

Her advice to me was first to be patient. But I had been patient for so long that I truly thought that I would die before I saw any change in our situation. She asked me what I wanted. I wanted action.

She said that I was to remember that she too wanted action. She wanted a divorce. Did I want that? I shrank back. That was decidedly not what I wanted. I wanted to expand my horizons. I wished to learn more about the world. I had a husband who was not perfect, but whose was? She informed me bitterly that her husband was considerably less than perfect. 'Grasp the day', was her next piece of advice. If a chance came along, take it.

I left her fully resolved to do just that. The next time that I was offered an opportunity to learn more I would not hesitate. With this in mind I went over to the home where my mother had died as I was due there to collect the remainder her possessions. Gathering together my mother's things and refusing to be downhearted at the fact that when she left this world they were so few, I talked to the woman who had informed me that my father had come back to see my mother as she lay dying. After some discussion she convinced me that she really had seen my father, or at least, his spirit. This prompted me to ask whether this sort of thing had ever happened before. Her eyes widened in astonishment.

"Oh yes."

"when?"

"Whenever someone dies, a relative who has gone before to the dreamtime comes back to guide them."

"But that's only for your tribe. It's not the same for us."

"Why is it not so?"

"Well, we are Christians."

"Is that your tribe?"

"Not exactly. It's our religion."

"Don't you have the dreamtime?"

"Why yes, we call it heaven. You go there if you are good."

"Who decides?"

"Who decides what?"

"Who decides if you are good?"

I was left speechless. I had never thought about this; and now an ignorant black woman of no education was opening my eyes. It made me angry.

"You don't know what you are talking about", I snapped.

"It very much sounds to me as if that is what I might say to you", she replied gently.

It was only later when I got home and was putting ma's things away that I cooled down and thought more about the dreamtime. Having pushed Pip into learning, and bearing in mind Mrs Wolstenholme's advice and example, I resolved that I too would find out more, so I went back and spoke again to the woman who had upset me.

"I'm sorry. I was cross with you and for no good reason. I should like to learn more about you and your people. I have heard enough to know that you all have tribes."

"Are you really interested or just idly curious?"

I swallowed my pride and sat down beside her.

"My mother was brought to this country forcibly and I was born here. I consider myself and my son to be Australians. I truly wish to learn more."

"My people have lived in this land since it began, having helped to create it through the singing. My mother was killed by a white man but my son lives with me and will be brought up in the beliefs of our tribe. We are the Bediagal. We come from near the place you call Parramatta, between there and the river."

Just at that moment Mrs Dujane was called away to work in the home. Her son Teildo smiled winningly at me as I said goodbye to her and I her asked if we might meet again.

"Come next week. Bring your son."

Our bookshop was doing well. Pip was employed and fully occupied all day so I felt free to go to see Mrs Dujane. I took Art with me and while he and Teildo played in the garden Mrs Dujane and I talked.

"How can you say that your people created this land by singing?"

"Who created it then?"

"Almighty God; he created everything."

"How do you know?"

"We have a book, the Bible, it says so."

"Who wrote the book?"

I paused and thought.

"I know not."

"It seems to me that you do not know many things."

"Whereas, I suppose you know everything."

"Olivia, would you be willing to come with me and learn, as I have, about the way we sang the land into being?"

"Yes, provided that I can be back by teatime to give my husband his tea."

This provoked a great bellow of laughter from Mrs Dujane who finally wiped tears from her eyes and said:

"No, if you came you would have to come for a while. It takes time to get wisdom."

Of course I refused. I went home, only to hear from Pip that he had been offered a special job that would take him away for a week. Could I manage while he was away? I knew that the shop practically ran itself. It seemed providential that Pip would be away so I could go off too. Something made me cautious. While agreeing that I could manage, I neglected to tell him that I too would not be at home. How I wished later on that I had not agreed so quickly with Mrs Dujane that I would go with her.

Art was now an inquisitive lively lad, full of mischief, like most boys, but unlike most, interested in learning. Where all the others were out playing or tormenting their sisters, he was in most times helping me. It came from me instructing him in whatever I was doing at the time. I had already taught him to read at quite an early age; so that by the time that he was six I launched him into Dickens, by the simple method of reading to him and getting him to follow what I was reading. That's one advantage of running a bookshop, there are always more copies of all the books than you would find in a normal home.

Then, when I had to go off to attend to some domestic duty, I would leave him to try to read where I had left off. This worked so well that we were soon reading a chapter each to each other alternately. One day he told me that he had already read the chapter that I was supposed to read next, and then I knew that I could leave him to read by himself. In the evenings we would talk about what he had read, and I, having already finished what he was reading, would add what I thought about the novel that he was reading.

In like fashion I taught him to write. I would write something down in the normal course of my work and I would get him to copy it. In due course I would set him a simple task such as making a list of all the books that had recently arrived and their price. From there it was easy to get him to write something about what he had read once he had finished reading a book. To begin with his efforts were very simple, but in no time at all he was writing quite elaborate offerings.

During all this time I carried on running the small bookshop while Pip worked elsewhere as the work became available. With his earnings and the takings from the shop we had a simple satisfactory life.

When I next met Mrs Dujane she seemed to have almost taken it for granted that I would want to go with here and would also be willing for Art to come with us.

"Olivia, if you wish to come with me I have to tell you that I am taking Teildo as he is growing up and needs to be educated. Would you be willing to bring Art?"

Something must have come over me for without any thought I said yes. Thinking about it later I wonder if Mrs Dujane had put something in my tea. She had offered me tea and I knew that it was not the sort that we normally had, but was bitter and aromatic. As we drank it together I saw her eyes over her cup and they expanded and contracted alarmingly just like the time Ma's eyes did when I had that fever. But maybe I am looking for excuses. If I had not gone with her I could have saved myself and Art so much trouble.

The following day I was packed. I took enough for a two day stay in that clearing near the river where Mrs Dujane said I was to camp with her, her son Teildo and my son Art. Now I think of it I must have been possessed. People who saw my preparations said that I was feverish and brushed aside any attempt to stop me and to make me think about what I was about to do. I told them that I was going to stay with Mrs Dujane and learn about the singing.

When we arrived in the clearing Teildo and Art immediately undressed and ran off together to bathe in the river. I took off some of my clothes and Mrs Dujane removed every stitch of hers and replaced them with bark strips. As it grew hotter and we sat under the trees listening to the chanting I too removed everything and, following everyone else's example I daubed myself with red mud. This immediately stopped insects biting me. I drank a potion and feeling slightly muzzy I lay down.

I fell asleep and when I woke up it was to find that I was being decorated with white and grey stripes and dots. Near me both Art and Teildo were similarly being decorated. I was alarmed as I saw they were both being given a spear each. It was explained to me that they needed these as they were to go walkabout and find their true selves in the land. I was encouraged to go to sleep and told that the following day a gathering of the clan would take place. It was further explained that both Art and I had been accepted into the clan as Mrs Dujane had sung us into it. No one called her Mrs Dujane; her name was Woolombo and my tribal name was Toomolo. Art had been renamed Domolo. None of this worried me in the slightest. It was as if I had shed my European skin like a snake sloughs off its outer covering, and as I did so I began to think and act more as a native.

Looking back now at my actions at this time I wonder if I had been tipped over into a mild form of dementia? Was it the sun? Was I drugged? Was I someone else? You might ask what I meant by this last question. I had read about people being more than one person. Was I such a case? Whatever the explanation, I was certainly not acting as I used to when I was younger.

Chapter 3

I watched the dancing and listened as Mrs Dujane explained to me a little of her world. She already knew about mine, and rejected much of it. Her robust denial of all that up to now I had taken for granted and believed in did not upset me in the least.

"We made the world by singing it into existence. I know that as I walk through the dust and mud and feel the rain as it falls upon me that one day my spirit will fly off to the great dreaming where my father and mother will be waiting to lead me home. That's my spirit. My body will go back into the earth mother where it will become other animals, maybe other people. The earth is sacred to us. Earth mother bears us and welcomes us back when we have done our time in this singing. We are given this life. It is a gift that we accept and cherish and it enables us to enter into a bond where, in exchange for our efforts we are allowed to use everything in the world to feed us and to clothe ourselves."

"How do you know all this? Is it written anywhere?"

"Why are you white people so concerned with writing? We are taught it from the beginning of our lives by listening to what our elders tell us. Our parents know that they have a sacred duty to tell us these things. It means that as we learn to live our lives we also learn why we are allowed to do so. We know that the country that you call Australia has always been here from the very first time that the sun rose. We are not like the white people who have just come. We have been here all along in the country. We know our land was given to us, so we have a sacred duty to protect it; we also have a sacred duty to protect all the animals that we share the land with.

"Who was it that gave you the land?"

Mrs Dujane looked sly.

"Different tribes have a different name for him. But what matters most is that the land is ours. We own it and live on it in the way that I have described to you."

"But I have seen lots of black people who do not live in this way."

"That's partly because they have been drawn away from the old ways. And, I must be honest, not all the old ways were good ones, some ways indeed were brutal. We needed to move away from them. Even before the white people came bad things happened. One trouble however is that although when the white people came and disliked our ways, some of which I now agree were wrong, they tended to dislike everything they saw. They did not stop and ask themselves why we behaved as we did; they simply assumed that we were ignorant."

I thought about my own experiences and how nakedness in natives had shocked me. I also remembered tales of natives being forced to wear clothes that I could see now would be unsuitable for this climate.

"So how are boys prepared? I can see how girls, by being with the women all day learn to be women."

"I cannot really tell you in full how the boys are initiated. Only a man can tell you that. It is forbidden for women to be involved. All I can say is that they go off together with their father or an older man and spend time in the bush. When they come back they are changed; they have become men, or at least they have set their feet on the path to becoming men."

"Can't I speak to one of the men and get them to tell me?"

Mrs Dujane looked alarmed. She glanced over to where some of the older men were sitting apart in the shade of a huge tree that was losing its bark.

"No, I'm sorry. You will have to rely on what I can tell you. You see, I am taking an enormous risk in bringing you and Art here. I do wish that we and the white people could be friends, but not all my tribe share this wish. There are some who are totally against this. They have tried to speak against the very idea, saying that we should remember the way we were hanged and forced off our land and introduced to drinking rum and other bad ways. I say that we should forget this if we are to exist in the future."

"Is that why you were so insistent that I should come with Arthur?"

Mrs Dujane hesitated.

"Maybe I was wrong to be so insistent. My time working amongst white people has changed me. I do love my tribe, but I can see their imperfections. At the same time that I'm pulled by the great serpent, I'm pulled the other way by what I have learned since I left my tribe. I cannot change everything of myself. I know that I would die inside if I were to try to do so."

Mrs Dujane looked sad. Her downcast looks contrasted vividly with the real happiness that came across in waves from the singing and dancing groups. A bird dance was succeeded by a wallaby dance, then as everyone used clapping sticks or stones to beat out the rhythm they all joined in. I could see Art and Teildo at the edge of the group. I had never before seen Art so enjoying himself.

It grew dark but the singing and dancing went on. As I watched a man came over to us and began to speak rapidly to Mrs Dujane. She waved at him angrily and he went away, but before he did so he looked at me. I didn't like the look that he gave me. I asked what had he wanted. Mrs Dujane said that he was an elder, always causing trouble, and this time he was insisting that the tribe's land should be returned to them. It grew late so I called Art over to me and we wrapped ourselves in blankets and laid ourselves down to sleep.

I was woken by thunder. I dressed quickly, washed my face in the stream and looked for Art. I packed up my things, making a roll of them so that I could carry them on my back. I called to Art who was playing with Teildo. He came reluctantly and I told him to get washed and dressed as we had to go home.

"Why can't I stay with Teildo?"

"Because we must return home."

"Why?"

"Because I say so. Now be a good lad and do as I say. Anyway your father will be returned soon and we must be home before he is."

He stood looking at me.

"Now, quickly get dressed."

He slowly and grudgingly pulled on his drawers and breeches. As he pulled his shirt over his head Teildo came to see what was happening.

"We are going to hunt. Aren't you coming too?"

He displayed a dead lizard that he had already caught.

"If you come with us you can join in the hunt for something bigger."

He swung the dead reptile invitingly at Art who flushed and turned to me.

"Can't I stay, please, please."

His face set into a stubborn replica of Pip's that I knew so well. His hands clenched into fists.

Mrs Dujane said:

"Oh let him. He'll be safe enough here with me."

"Oh! Very well, just for a little while more. I must go home, but I will come back to collect you this evening."

He shouted in triumph, pulling off his clothes. I felt a mixture of pride and annoyance.

I reached home just after Pip got there. He had come in and Lizbeth had made him his tea. She had gone home leaving him to eat it and read the paper. I could see that something had upset him. So having had my tea too, I settled down to wait, knowing that he would tell me in his own good time what it was that was on his mind. But before he did so he asked where Art was. When I told him he was so angry. I do not think that I have ever seen him look so angry as he was on this occasion.

"In God's name Liv, what do you think you are playing at?"

He then told me that there was a difficult situation at work and that he had to back immediately to deal with it. He would not tell me what it was about. Instead he told me to get hold of the carter that we used to collect stock from the docks, and go straight away with him to collect Art.

Luckily the carter was available, so as soon as Pip went off I was able to direct the carter to where I had left Art. As we went along he told me that there had been trouble with the blacks who were getting above themselves.

"Someone will have to teach them a lesson. They must be shown who is in charge of this land now."

Chapter 4

We reached the spot where I had left Art and I asked the carter to wait while I went into the bush through the trees.

"Watch out for snakes", he called as he led his horse into the shade.

I wiped off the sweat that ran down my face. I walked out of the hot bright sunlight into the shadow of the trees. For a moment I was almost blind as my eyes took a while to adjust to the darkness. I looked around. Was I in the right place? This was surely the place where I had left Art and all the others in the morning. I stood shocked. The place was totally deserted, everyone and everything gone. I called out in alarm. I ran to the edge of the stream. I panicked until I found Art's clothes in a bundle. I took comfort from the fact that they were folded carefully.

Behind me the carter who had heard my cry, and had come to join me, said:

"Where is he then?"

I shook my head as I grasped the bundle of clothes.

"He should be here. They all should be here."

"So where have the bastards gone then? You can't trust them you know. Have they taken him?"

I wanted to scream that I didn't know. I shook as if I had the ague. I tried to control my trembling. I tried to do the same with my breathing. I forced myself to think. What had they said? Why were they not here? The carter spat dismissively.

"Well, what now?

The bushes stirred and opened. A totally naked black man stood there. We had not heard him approach. The carter stepped back visibly alarmed. His already ruddy face became a darker shade. I stepped forward. I recognised the man. He was one of the group that had kept themselves apart during the singing and dancing when I had been with the tribe earlier. The carter recovered his nerve and stamped forward in his long boots made from kangaroo leather. He shouted angrily:

"Were is her boy? What have you done with him you black heathen bastard?

The black man stood still. He looked with contempt at the carter, then he shifted his gaze to me.

"You want your boy?"

"Yes, of course I do. Where is he?"

"We want our land."

I stood in despair.

"I know nothing about your land."

He gestured imperiously. He waved majestically in an encompassing movement saying as he did so:

"All this is ours. We want it back."

"I haven't taken it."

He shrugged and turned away and began to move back into the bush.

"Wait, wait."

He stopped. He turned. He waited. What in God's name could I say to stop him?

"I will talk to…"

He waited. I didn't know who I could talk to, then I thought about John Adam. His name was the only one that I could dredge up from sludge that my mind had suddenly become.

"I will talk to John Adam."

"John Adam?"

"Yes", I gabbled, "He's an important man."

The black man stood impassively. Insects buzzed around me lighting on my sweaty face and arms. I brushed them off. I tried not to look at his sexual parts. I grew hotter from the heat and the shame of seeing his nakedness. I felt the sweat trickle down my legs.

The carter coughed and we heard his horse stamp on the hard sun baked earth.

"Yes, You go and talk to this John man. Come back tomorrow with papers."

"What papers?"

"Papers to give us back our land."

I threw up my hands. I stood helplessly. I knew that it was hopeless. Nothing could be done so quickly.

"I want to see my son."

"He is well. He is happy. He is learning to be a real man."

For the first time he smiled, not a malicious smile, but a friendly one. The carter took my arm saying:

"You can't trust them. They are bloody savages."

"I have to", I said sharply shaking off his hand.

Chapter 5

I cried as we went back in the cart. The carter grumbled about the blacks throughout the journey. Before we arrived home I made him promise that he would tell no one. I was frightened that if people that we knew heard about this they would get angry and possibly try to attack the blacks and this would prevent me from getting Art back.

Pip was still out. I knew that he had gone back to work to deal with the problem that had worried him so much, so I thought that I ought to go straightaway down to see John Adam. Lizbeth was helping in the shop, and Leonard Butler was at home in his room so I knew that could safely go out.

Catching one of the horse trams that were soon to give way to more modern ones I rode down to John Adam's office. Elaine Pomeroy was still working there and, as I had known her all my life, she made it possible for me to see him straight away. Knowing how loose a tongue she had normally I tried to mask my feelings and I said nothing but I suspected that my reddened eyes betrayed me. She certainly looked at me suspiciously.

John Adam's son Federico, known to all as Freddy, was now John's main reason for living. His marriage was a disaster but the Italian bitch, as Pip used to call her, at least stayed with him. Pip averred that she only did so because of the money. So I knew that my trouble with Art would not be lightly put aside. John adored his only son and knew that I was as doting a mother as he was a father.

I was right to assume that John Adam would be ready to listen to me and to help me. His love for his difficult son made him sensitive to my problem and my feelings for mine. He listened to my story without commenting upon how stupid I had been. My hopes that he would be able to do something immediately about the land were totally dashed however when he said there was absolutely no possibility of anything being done in that quarter.

He said this sadly as we sat together in his sumptuous office, the symbol of the progress that he had made in having created a financial empire despite being the son of a poor tailor in Melbourne. He left his chair, came round his desk and sat beside me. He was much greyer than I remembered him being, and much less steady on his feet. I knew that he was now drinking moderately, having been warned by his doctor that his previous life had to be moderated so his unsteadiness was probably just old age.

I cried. I felt that the one chance that I might have had to rescue Art was slipping away. He regarded me as I wept. He waited for me to compose myself. I thought that he would have acted immediately just as he did when he rescued my Ma. Now he was wasting time.

"John", I said, "if we don't go back tomorrow..."

"Olivia. We shall go back tomorrow. I promise you that, but we shall go to parley with them."

I was aghast. I struggled to speak coherently.

"Parley?"

"Precisely. They have something of yours. You want it back. They want something from us in return, something that we are in no position to give them. They do not know that. Nevertheless we shall enter into discussions. Where there is life there is always hope. And, do believe me dearest Olivia, your Art is alive. He is their one hope of us helping them, so they are caring for him as well as you or I might care for our sons ourselves."

"So you think Art is safe?"

"Totally sure. Arthur is their bargaining counter. You were right to keep this quiet by the way. We do not want a bunch of ignorant men trampling in and scaring them off. So say nothing to anyone except Pip of course. Remember that, no one, absolutely no one. I will send you word about how we shall meet to morrow. Now go home."

I left his room not really sure that I had done all that I could. I felt so guilty. As I did so, Elaine, gave me a look of such concern that cut right through my resolve to speak to no one, and almost weakened my determination not to tell her all. I felt that I had to tell her about my trouble. She had been my route to John. I owed it to her to be frank. She put a hand upon my arm and looked at me. She did not have to say anything. I was about to tell her everything when John came out and stood there quietly. I took my hand away and said goodbye quietly and left.

Elaine was not one to give up that easily. When her day's work was over she came to see me. Elaine had reached that age when you do not change very much. She looked her age but carried it off with a liveliness that many a younger woman envied. She was also skilled at wheedling out secrets So that evening we sat together drinking tea and I told her everything, starting with Ma's death when I had been told that my father had appeared. Up to now I had been careful as to whom I had imparted this information. I went on to tell her how I had so foolishly put Art into danger. Her reaction was that I should tell the police straight away. She said that they would know what to do and I would soon have Art back. I demurred. John had told me that he thought that we could get a better result by doing it ourselves. Besides, I had seen how the police acted, frequently rushing in and upsetting everything and everybody.

Chapter 6

"We will use Walloomba."

I must have shown how incredulous I felt.

"He will be fine."

"How can he be? Every time I have seen him he has been drunk."

"That's because he has nothing to do, nothing upon which to exercise his skills. We will employ him to do what he does best."

"And that is..?"

"Tracking. He will find Arthur for us. No matter where he is."

I hesitated.

"So you think we shall be able to find him?"

My hesitation was because I really wanted to ask John whether he thought Art was still alive. I felt a bubble of hysteria rise inside me. I fought it down. It returned as I thought of Walloomba lying in a drunken stupor outside our shop. We had tried to employ him in the past. He took our money and bought grog. We tried giving him food instead of money, but he always managed to get strong drink of some sort or another from somewhere or someone. Even my husband, Phillip, who had embraced alcohol in the past with a fervour never surpassed by any convert to a religion, had been critical of the natives who seemed unable to cope with life unless they were full of grog.

"You can take Jack King too."

"Jack King? I don't know him, do I? Isn't he...?

"Yes, one of my men on whom I rely to get things done. Believe me, Olivia, he will be very useful."

He rang a bell on his desk and told the girl who came in to send for Jack King. At first I was so bound up with my feelings that I sat twisting my kerchief in my hands until I realised that Jack had entered the room and both men were looking at me. I had completely missed what John had said.

He was introduced to me and then turned away to get his instructions from John. I looked at him. Compared to Phillip he was small and wiry. He had a tough outdoor look to him, and yet his clothes were those of a dandy; they were certainly much more expensive that I would have expected to see on the back of a hired man. Clearly Jack King was something more. Clean-shaven with a moustache below pronounced cheekbones, some might say that he was almost handsome, well, let's say attractive anyway. I particularly noticed his abundant hair that was carefully swept back from a broad forehead.

Chapter 7

I had underestimated Elaine Pomeroy's loose tongue; I should have remembered how she loved to pass on any gossip that came her way. The truth is that she had very little else in her life, so she lived vicariously through others. Indeed in the past we all had enjoyed her racy accounts of John's wife's behaviour. Marietta was an Italian who saw no reason to curb her excitable behaviour to suit her husband, so Elaine had plenty of grist for her mill.

I know that I should have listened to John's warning, but I was weak and telling her everything gave me some comfort. The first that I knew that she had betrayed my confidence was when the police came to see me. A large sergeant with a big moustache and a hectoring manner called and said that he had come in connection with the disappearance of a boy. He wanted to know whether my boy, he consulted a notebook at this point to check the name, but before he could say another word I stopped him.

"There has obviously been a mistake. My boy is on a holiday."

"Your boy, Arthur Gargery, is not missing?"

"No, as I said, he is with some friends."

Looking relieved, he folded up his notebook, putting it into a pocket that he buttoned up tight with a silver button that shone brightly. It twinkled in the hot sunlight as he said:

"I'm most pleased to hear that. We heard that he was in some sort of trouble with those black bastards. Mind you, if he is in trouble and you come whining to us later on I'm not at all sure that we shall be quick to assist you."

Saying this, he hefted his not inconsiderable bulk out of my best armchair, thanked me for the tea, and left.

Chapter 8

I was caught in the mesh of the net of my own lies. I had denied that Art had been taken from me for what I considered to be the best of reasons: I feared that our plans to rescue him would be upset by the clumsy efforts of others. So I denied the truth. Now I had to continue in that lie. It meant, of course, that I could expect no help from the authorities. We were on our own. If everything worked out well that would be fine. I just did not like to think of an alternative ending to our endeavour.

So we set out. I was in a depressed mood. It was impossible to judge how Walloomba was feeling but Jack had told me that Walloomba was confident that finding Art would be easy. I hoped that he was right.

The only thing that raised my spirits slightly was the fact that I had Jack King as well as Walloomba. Jack was a man who had spent much of his life in the wilder parts of Australia. He had been employed by John Adam in the past on all sorts of situations where he had come in contact with the black natives. He seemed to understand them to certain extent. His attitude to them was still tinged however with a measure of contempt for them and their behaviour.

He was dismissive of blacks in general and Walloomba in particular. He saw him as a typical example of the drunken broken down shells of men that he had encountered throughout his travels. I tried to defend Walloomba, saying that he had tracking skills that would be useful to us. Jack spat in the dust before saying that just because they were here when we arrived and tried to civilise them, and just because they seemed to know their way around the little piece of land that they laid claim to, they pretend that they have skills that he very much doubted they really had.

We had stopped and were resting in the shade. It was overpoweringly hot. Just to move made us sweat. To add to that, I was unused to being out in this way. I had always tried in the past to avoid being outside in the sun. I was naturally pale and I had worked hard at maintaining my complexion. Now I could feel that I was red and blotchy.

Jack wore his hat; it was the one that he wore habitually. I can't remember ever seeing him outside without it. I wore one too. It was absolutely essential to have your head covered up against the fierce heat of the Australian sun, and yet the natives walked about bareheaded. Jack said that that they had no sense and so had no feeling. Walloomba sat in the sun, his almost bare head with little tufts of wool-like hair, glistening in the sun. We had stopped at his insistence to talk to a group of mangy looking blacks who shuffled away from us looking at us suspiciously. Walloomba waved me a warning to keep back.

We sat in the shade and I listened to Jack moaning on about the fact that we were losing time. Eventually I could stand it no longer so I stood up, but before I could go over to the blacks they all stood up too and melted away just like black ink running into a river. One minute they were there, and the next they had gone. Walloomba, smiling, came towards me.

He looked cooler than I felt. He was not only bareheaded, but had nothing on his feet. He scuffed them through the hot sandy soil making me feel even hotter. Over his shoulder he carried a bag made from some sort of animal skin. That was all that he carried. Everything he owned was in that bag. Consequently he was able to move much quicker than we could. I began to wonder who was the most sensible member of our party. He was certainly no longer drunk. When we started out he had swayed about making Jack exclaim with annoyance. Only the fact that John Adam insisted that Walloomba had to accompany us had persuaded Jack to let him stay.

He pointed to an area where Jack had said previously that we would never find Art.

"Come. Now. We go there."

Jack's expression became more than just dislike and bordered on hatred.

"You black heathen bastard. I've already said that we won't find him there. There's no water, no shade, no food nothing but sand and rock and scrub. I know I've been there. You just want us to get lost."

He turned to me as Walloomba stood impassively.

It's desert there, nothing but bloody desert, there's nothing there. We won't find Art there. Remember what happened to the people on that expedition, to Wills and to Burke.

He turned away from Walloomba clenching his fists and looking into my face. I took a step back. He followed me almost spitting his words into my face in his anger.

"Listen to me. I was there. At least I was at the edge of it. It was a complete disaster. They have covered up most of what went wrong to hide the guilt of the men who should never have allowed it to happen. I know what can happen, what can slide into chaos if you go somewhere where you shouldn't be."

What an odd choice of words, I thought. I knew that he had considerable experience, but I hadn't realised that he had been involved in the great Victorian Expedition 1860. His final comment ' somewhere where you shouldn't be' stayed in my mind. It was the 'shouldn't be' that intrigued me.

"Look, Olivia, let's stay here tonight and I'll explain."

He had certainly changed his tune. Now, instead of wanting to go on, he wanted us to wait. I called to Walloomba who had moved away to come back. I asked him whether we should stay at least one night. He looked at me gravely, all trace of the former boozy black man burned out by the sun and the exertion. He nodded slowly, the surprised me by saying:

"You must hear what this man has to tell you, tomorrow we can continue."

Still torn between remaining and insisting that we went on, for I was desperate to see my son, I hesitated. Walloomba put a very warm black hand upon my shoulder. Behind me I sensed Jack bristling with suppressed fury.

"Your son is in good hands, believe me."

Wallomba withdrew his hand, slowly turned, and walked away.

"The black bastard. If he as much as puts a finger on you again, he will have me to deal with."

"Jack. Jack, stop it. We will get nowhere if you constantly see trouble where there is none."

Later that evening, once we had eaten a frugal meal that mostly consisted of oatmeal, I asked Jack to tell me more about the expedition. I knew something about it, of course, despite being young at the time, as Ma had read about it in a newspaper that she had collected. She always maintained that a newspaper was in nowise diminished by having been read, so it made sense to read one that someone else had bought and discarded. This particular one was the Argus and came to her wrapped around some books that she had ordered from Melbourne. I shared her thrifty common-sense approach to life and wished that she could have been here with us now; I could well do with her support.

Jack told me that John King had been his uncle. This was the famous John King, the only survivor of the expedition. Jack had been desperate to be involved, but so many wanted to go he never stood a chance. He had assisted in the preparations; these were the ones that Ma had read about. He had also seen them set off. What's more he had seen his uncle on his return. Then, later on when his uncle was very ill, and just before he died, Jack heard the whole unvarnished story. Jack would visit him and sit with him, and gradually his uncle would draw upon his memories and tell his nephew what exactly had happened.

Walloomba joined us. Jack glared at him. Walloomba squatted down and said:

"I know you."

To my surprise, Jack flinched and looked away.

I looked at Jack, my face a question.

"Yes," he confirmed.

"We know each other."

"From the time of the expedition?"

"No. It was later."

"Later?"

"Yes, much longer after the expedition. It was doomed you know. Lots of people thought that. Mind you, most never said anything until well after the whole fiasco, then there were mutterings about pride going before a fall."

"Ah! Now that sounds like one of my mother's sayings. She had a saying for every situation you know."

"Yes, I know. She said 'Least said soonest mended' when I brought her home that time."

"You brought her home?" When was this?

"I rescued her. Brought her back to your place in a cab."

A dim memory swam back slowly into my mind. How Toby had run to tell John, and he had sent someone immediately to fetch her safely back home when she was in danger of being taken up; and a memory of my being so relieved that I hardly took any notice of who had been with her. I remembered going upstairs to my room above the bookshop and crying with relief in my room.

"Yes, better educated people than I was at that time used to talk of hibris."

"Hubris", I corrected him.

"Just so. Hubris."

Chapter 9

I was about to say something more about hubris and nemesis when Walloomba interrupted us. He waved to the group of blacks that he had been speaking to, and they stirred and pointed to the north. I waited to hear what he had learned. I was feeling low. I was losing any feelings of optimism that I had had. I was bitten by insects and the bites had swollen. I tried not to scratch them, but it was difficult to keep my fingers away from what, in some cases were becoming weeping sores.

"What have you found out?" I asked listlessly.

"Your son has been seen."

I sat up. My heartbeat increased. I became breathless.

"Is he here?"

"No. He was here but, they have gone up the river."

I slumped back. I ached and itched and nearly cried from vexation and pain. I wanted to scratch and scratch. Jack was watching me.

"It's good news. We know where he is going at least."

"How can you say that? How do you know that?"

He replied patiently:

"They are going up the river, so we can follow them by doing the same."

To do that we needed a boat. I fretted as Jack and Walloomba negotiated with the natives. It seemed to take forever. I walked away from them towards the group of half naked women who smiled in welcome as I squatted down beside them and their children. They spoke to me and I shook my head in the universally accepted indication that I did not understand. A very young girl was pushed towards me. She spoke shyly in English.

"You look for your boy, your son?"

The women beamed and clapped their hands in approval.

She became even shyer and tried to turn away. She was prodded back to face me.

"Yes, yes. Have you seen him?"

She turned a beautiful face towards me. She whispered:

"You are mother of pale boy, so high?" indicating with her had the height that Art was.

"Yes, yes. Have you seen him?"

She twisted her fingers together and twitched her toes in the dust.

"He was here. Now he is gone."

An older woman whose pendulous breasts and nakedness would have offended me once, but no longer shocked me, spoke to the girl. She put a tentative hand on my arm. She pointed to one of my inflamed insect bites with as black a finger as mine were white

"Hurting?"

"Yes, very much."

She turned back and spoke rapidly. The women all began to speak at once. The older woman raised her arm in an unspoken comment. They all fell silent. Incongruously I thought of Caroline Chisholm and the way she dominated proceedings and people. What would she and Estella have thought about me now, sitting bedraggled, skin mottled with weeping sores and wearing infinitely less than a lady ought to be wearing? Where was my bonnet? Where were my stays, my chemise?

I was pulled to my feet and urged towards the edge of the clearing away from Jack and Walloomba who were still talking to the black men. I watched as the women gathered leaves and put them into a small pot together with some river water. Ma's words came back to me. How Lady Spens had collected herbs when she first came to Australia. I wish that I had listened more to Ma when she talked about those times. I have found though that it's not until someone dies that you begin to wish that you had asked them about their life. When they die they take it all with them, unless they manage to set it down in some fashion.

I do remember how she told me that after she was rescued from Parramatta she went to live with Amanda Jane before she became Lady Spens, and how Amanda Jane learned from Jonas, their black boy, how to use herbs to keep away troublesome insects. She also told me that Amanda Jane collected all kinds of herbs and fruits and with them she made cordials and physics to treat the animals and the people who made up their small establishment. She went to live in as a servant, and this meant that Amanda Jane had more time to collect herbs.

When the natives had boiled the leaves they took them and bound them on to where the insect bites were suppurating. Immediately they felt better and as the day went on I felt better too. They gave me a pot of the boiled herbs and the little girl who had quickly lost her shyness, and was now ready to be an apt interpreter, told me how to use the potion and the leaves.

When Jack and Wallooma finally managed to buy a small boat we set out, with both the men paddling and me sitting in the stern. I constructed a sort of shelter so that I was shaded from the worst of the sun. We made good progress as the river ran smoothly between banks of vegetation and large trees.

It started to rain. Really heavy rain, the sort that I had seen several times before when rivers had broken their banks and houses and land had been washed away. I had been warned several times by people who knew about these things that as we had only been in the country for a relatively short while we could not really comprehend what sort of weather was normal. We had only arrived here in 1788. It was now 1889. Who knows what the country had been like for the hundreds of years before we arrived?

After a day we camped and I used more of the herbal mixture. In the morning we set out again, and as we did so it began to rain yet again. Gradually it began to rain more heavily. I gave up using the sun shelter that I had adapted to keep off the rain and helped by bailing out the bottom of the boat using the pot that I had been given. The river rose. It was a slow rise at first, then abruptly it became a streaming foaming torrent that quickly overflowed the banks. The rain continued in intensity and soon it was impossible to see precisely where the river banks were. It was only by steering between the trees that lined the banks that we were able to continue.

Then in a moment it stopped and it became hot and steamy. Snakes of all sizes slid through the water moving through the debris brought down the river by the rain.

Something white caught my eye. I called to Jack who manoeuvred the boat so that we could get alongside it. I fished it out, untangling it from pieces of wood. It was a shirt, and one that I recognised. The last time that I had seen it Art had been taking it off.

"It's Art's", I said

Jack grinned.

"You see, I knew we had reason to be hopeful," he replied.

"It obviously got washed away when the river flooded. Good thing that you spotted it. Now we know that we are getting near them."

We pushed on greatly encouraged by our find. I carefully folded up the shirt and put it with my other meagre belongings. While I was doing this we heard the sound of rushing water and after we rounded a great stand of gum trees we found that the river ahead was now a great cataract.

"That's that then", said Jack.

"We can't use the boat any longer. We can't carry it over that lot," he added as he nodded towards the rushing water.

We tied the boat to a tree making sure that it was sufficiently near the river, as we hoped to return this way, and it would have been a disaster to find the boat high and dry and yards away from the river. Once again on foot we picked our way over the rocks that were steaming in the hot sun. Birds screamed and fought over the dead bodies of animals that had been caught in the flood.

"You see how nature ensures that everything gets tidied up?" said Jack.

Walloomba nodded in agreement.

"The great serpent has arranged everything in the world. Everything has its place. Everything has its work to do. Soon the ants will finish what the birds have begun."

Saying this he led the way into a small clearing where he quickly pulled away some debris to reveal a rock. At the back of the rock was a small cliff and he pointed to some carvings on it. With a scarred black finger he traced the outline of a great snake.

"Jesus! That's some snake. It must have been there for some time too. Look how worn it is", said Jack, who for once looked quite awestruck.

"It was put there longer ago than any of us can remember. It was put there when time began", said Walloomba proudly.

"Now you begin to see why we own the land. The great serpent gave it to us to look after, and he made us put him here on the rock to remind us to care for it."

Despite what was obviously a sacred place, Walloomba quite readily assented to our making camp there for the night. I quickly realised that Jack's awe and my respect meant that we were not encroaching upon the sacredness. In fact, in some peculiar way we were adding to it.

I slept for a while by the side of the fire that Walloomba had lit. I have no idea how he produced a fire but he did so by twirling sticks, then suddenly there was a flame and then a cheerful blaze.

As we sat there we heard a rustling in the bush. By now I was sufficiently used to being in the bush and hearing all sorts of noises but what came out of the nearest bushes amazed me.

Chapter 10

It was Mrs Dujane! She calmly walked into the light of the fire and stood there.

We all stood up, Jack reaching for his gun, but Walloomba, pushing it down, and smiling broadly, said:

"I wondered if my message had got to you."

"Yes, but it has taken me some days to get back to you."

She turned to me and said:

"Your son is safe. I left him quite fit and well."

"Where is he?"

"He is with some of my people.   I think that it's time that I revealed who I really am."

"I thought you were Mrs Dujane."

She smiled. She looked directly at me.

"I am Yellow Alice."

I made no response.

"I was Miss King."

"I'm sorry, but neither of those names mean anything to me."

She turned to Jack.

"They mean something to you though, don't they?"

He bowed his head in assent. His face was hidden so I couldn't gauge his feelings no matter how hard I looked. I guessed from his posture however that he was not pleased that Mrs Dujane was telling me this.

"He knows my history", she said bitterly, " because he is part of it.

"The man that everyone thought so well of; the man who was the only survivor of that great Victorian expedition to discover what was already known by the people who lived there was my father!"

"John King?"

"Yes, John King."

"I find that very difficult to believe."

"So now you are calling me a liar."

"No, not at all. I'm just so taken aback at what you are saying."

"Listen then. When John King, my father, was near to death he was cared for by the Yandruwandha tribe. This was one of the tribes that tried to help the expedition. Not many people realise that throughout the whole time that the expedition was blundering along the local tribes were constantly watching them and sending messages about them to each other."

"Messages? How could they do that?"

"We would send smoke signals. We have other methods too. How do you suppose that Walloomba reached me and brought me here?

The members of that expedition were offered assistance; they were invited to join in the corroborees; they were offered gunyahs. Everything was refused, even our food, except at the very end when they had to accept it.

Finally when only John King was left, and left so helpless after the deaths of his companions, he was taken to a gunyah where he was cared for. In time he recovered sufficiently to take a part in everyday tribal matters. He helped get food for he still had his gun. And he took the Yandruwandha woman that was offered him. She was my mother and John King was my father, and I was known as Yellow Alice. I think my father would have called me Alice, but the Yellow was added to my name as my complexion was not as dark as that of the other Yandruwandha girls.

I was born in 1862 and Jack here knows what happened after my first few years in the tribe. When I was ten I was brought to Melbourne to be a house servant, and I must say that I was well treated. I was taught to read and write and encouraged to forget my upbringing. You can have no idea how difficult it was for me to wear boots. For ten years I had gone barefoot. Now I was forced to put on leather boots that were an agony to me. If I was ever in trouble it was usually because I had abandoned my footwear to enjoy being close to the earth."

Jack got up and stirred up the fire. Sparks flew up. His face looked troubled.

"Three years after I arrived in Melbourne I was taken to Sydney where a Mrs Kaye employed me in her Home for old people. I expect that you know about that woman and her dark past?"

I shook my head. I knew that Ma knew something about Mrs Kaye but I never discovered what it was.

"I got married to a man in the Bediagal tribe. I now consider myself to be of that tribe. I had a son, and he is to all intents and purposes a Bediagal. When I met you I was still employed at the Home and seeing your interest in how we lived, I thought that I would help you to understand more about us. But the elders thought that if I could persuade you to come with me they could take your son and use him to bargain over their lost lands."

Jack snorted dismissively.

"They never had any claim to land. Before we came to this country all the blacks simply moved about all over it. No one owned it. Then, when we arrived it was taken over in the name of Queen Victoria. If anyone owns anything, she does."

Mrs Dujane stayed quiet for a moment, then said slowly and determinedly:

"You are a clever man. Clever men do not know everything however."

She moved back and the light of the fire shone clearly on the carving of the great serpent that seemed to writhe and move as the flickering light fell on it. Jack said nothing at first. Then he seemed to gather his thoughts together. He spoke as slowly and deliberately as she had:

"Right. I accept that this carving proves that you have been here some time. I accept that. I expect Mrs Gargery accepts that.   But you don't know what you are up against. You might think that you have a moral right to ownership of the land, but there are clever people, lawyers and suchlike who can prove with their bits of paper that they have a legal right. I can assure you, and I speak from bitter experience, that legal rights win out every time over   moral rights.

When I was taken on by Adam and Pirrip, I was supposed to be interviewed by Mr Pirrip, but he was away, so John Adam saw me instead. He explained to me that recent discoveries in England and in Australia of minerals and other items had interested him. He asked me what was the driving force in Australia, but before I could answer he told me that it was, or would be, railways. He went on to tell me how England was being transformed by railways, how in the Russian War the eventual result was influenced by the building of a railway to move essential supplies.

He spoke with passion about this, and, young as I was, I still knew enough not to stop him, despite my unclear understanding why he was telling me this. He went on to say that railways needed iron and coal, and that he thought that I could help him find coal and iron ore in the Australian outback!

Apparently, following his investment in the great , vsole survivor I could find out from him what the expedition had discovered in the way of geological finds. I had to disappoint him. I told him that I was unlikely to be able to talk to my uncle as I was estranged from the family. This made him pause and think. He sent me away, telling me to return the following afternoon."

Mrs Dujane moved impatiently and clearly wanted to interrupt.

"No", I said, forestalling her. "Let him finish. I want to hear this."

Jack looked at me gratefully and went on:

"The next day he saw me alone and put to me what I could only describe as an amazing idea. He had brooded overnight and had come to the following conclusion: just as Abel Magwitch had made a gentleman, he would make someone similar, but more useful than an ornamental gentleman! He commented that if a transported convict could create a gentleman, a son of a tailor could make a professional geologist.

I couldn't stop myself. I had to say it.

"It's what Ma said. It's the Magwitch effect!"

Mrs Dujane said drily:

""So, you tell me not to interrupt! Now I think we both should let him finish."

Jack stirred the fire again and a again a shower of sparks shot up. This time his face looked less troubled and more angry.

"I'm not so sure that you will be pleased to hear the rest of my story. John Adam's plan was to ensure that I was instructed in the latest details about that science and that I would then secretly put it to use on his behalf. I queried the need for secrecy. His answer was that whatever I found out would be valuable. If I found deposits of iron ore or coal I was to report to him and no one else, and he would arrange to buy or get hold of the land where I had found it.

I was completely taken aback by this, but John Adam is a forceful man, and when he has set his mind to something he sees it through to the end. So I did as I was bid. He did as he had promised and I was shortly either being instructed or was reading journals and books to assist me. To cover our tracks I was employed as a general hand whose task was to go around seemingly to keep a weather eye out for trouble in the Adam and Pirrip Empire. This gave me plenty of scope to roam further afield and I was occasionally lucky as I not only studied the rudiments of geology, but having tried with some success to learn some of the tribal languages, I found the blacks were willing to talk to me. They would show me areas where they knew I was interested in the rocks. God alone knows what they thought of his madman who would spend hours or even days with them talking about their land. I knew that were I to find anything we would take the land from them, but I thought at that time that they are such God-awful lazy fellows that I had no feelings of guilt on that score."

I had listened to what Mrs Dujane had to say and to Jack's story of how he had come to be employed by John Adam with growing impatience. I could begin to see how what had happened in the past might have led us to where we were now, but I was concerned with only one thing in the present: where was Art? Turning to Mrs Dujane, I asked her where Art was now, and was he well? She told me once again that he was in good health and in good spirits, and that she would lead us to him.

Chapter 11

I could see that Jack was not happy at following Mrs Dujane, but Walloomba persuaded him that this was our best chance of catching up with Art and getting him out of the clutches of the tribal elders. Jack said that even if we were to get to Art we would still have to negotiate with them. I replied that we would just have to cross that bridge when we came to it. As I said this, a vivid memory of my mother saying this came into my head. 'My God' I thought, 'I'm beginning to turn into my mother!'

And so we set out. I was much more cheerful now and chattered with Jack to try to cheer him up. He remained morose, almost sullen whilst Walloomba, to my surprise, seemed anxious. He constantly looked behind us as if expecting to us to be followed. When I asked him what was worrying him, he shook his head. I could not make out whether that was because there was nothing to worry about, or simply his way of indicating that I was not to worry.

We made good progress as Mrs Dujane seemed to know exactly where she was going. Then, after a short pause to rest, she pointed to some rocky outcrops and said that we had to climb now. When he saw them Jack swore which made me laugh.

So we climbed, using all our energy to get through the broken ground that was littered with rock and scrub. As we climbed small lizards ran away from us. Once we disturbed a snake that was sunning itself on the hot rocks.

Jack was as considerate as any gentleman could be. Several times he held my hand to pull me up a difficult section. At the last steep difficult slope I almost gave up. It was like rock climbing. Then he simply clasped me around the waist and pushed me up until I was able to stand on the summit. I didn't have to say anything, as my grateful look was surely enough. In any case I was so out of breath so speech was impossible. I squeezed his hand in thanks though. Having done so I quickly removed it for there was more than concern in his face. I can still feel his arm about me, even after all this time.

At the summit of a small hillock Mrs Dujane stopped and said that we were now to wait. Even she found it hot, so we all moved together into the shade of the few stunted gum trees that poked out from cracks in the broken rocks. I asked Mrs Dujane what we were waiting for. She raised her hand to caution me to silence. We all listened and heard the sound of something, or someone coming our way. She looked anxious and spoke sharply to Walloomba who spoke briefly, and it seemed defensively in return. Again we listened. The noise was louder now, and it was being made by more than one thing or one person.

We were all looking back at the way in which we had come, so we almost missed the small figure that appeared on the cliff ahead of us. It was only when he yelled out and waved to us that we swung round, ignoring whatever or whoever was coming toward us from the rear.

He was only there for a moment but I was sure that it was Art. As he waved to us some black men appeared and led him away. I was about to spring up and climb up to where we had seen him when behind us a voice said:

"Right, so you've led us a merry dance, but you can give us the paper now."

Chapter 12

"Come on. The bloody paper, and be quick about it", went on a short white man whose face was bright red from having toiled his way, along with another man, up the rocks after us.

The two of them were armed with guns that they made sure that we could clearly see. I ignored them, turning to ask Mrs Dujane if the figure that we had seen was Art. She had gone. I turned to Walloomba and asked:

"What is happening? What is going on? Who are these men? Do you know?"

"All right. All right. Don't get excited", said the short white man, his face a little less flushed than it had been before.

"We've been sent to collect the papers. He wants the paper back, that's all. Give us the paper and we will go. You can collect your kid and come home as soon as you like then."

He smiled revealing broken teeth and went on:

"We know Yellow Alice has the documents. You do know that she is really Yellow Alice, don't you?"

I said that she had told us about her early life, but I couldn't see what that had to do with me and my son.

The short white man let out an exasperated sigh.

"What were you going to do up here?"

Jack took him by the arm and led him away speaking rapidly to him. He listened carefully. Jack came back.

"Listen to me now. These men have been sent by John Adam to follow us. It seems that we have all been fooled by

71

Mrs Dujane, because she already has the documents that the tribe need to show that they still own the land."

"Why if she already has the deeds did she insist on dragging us out here?"

"It's rather complicated, but I believe that she wanted me, on John Adam's behalf, to be seen to hand them over; she really wanted John himself to do it."

"So what happens now?"

"I think that I have persuaded these men that she will come back which will give them the opportunity to take back the papers. I told them that she would come back to the corroboree. That means that we can wait here to see what Mrs Dujane wanted us to see."

We sat in the increasing heat listening to the screaming of the birds that seemed to have been disturbed for they flew above the cliffs in great flocks. On the cliff opposite us we saw a small figure appear. It looked like Art but I couldn't be sure if it was. Behind us there was a collective murmur from the women. With the sun behind the figure it was difficult to see clearly. He, for it seemed to be a boy, appeared to be pale. He was certainly Art's size and he had his slender build, but then all the native boys were slight in build and stature.

He raised his arms. I thought that he was waving to us. I began to raise my arm to wave back when there was a sudden report from our left and a slight puff of smoke that revealed from where the shot had come, for it was indeed a shot. The figure on the cliff sank down and then toppled forward as we all gasped or cursed or, in my case simply screamed.

I pressed forward trying to see where he had landed. There were too many bushes. I pushed through these lacerating my arms and hands as I did so. I pressed on disregarding any pain. I would have pressed on even further and probably toppled myself into the gulch between our two cliffs had not the women, who were chanting in a strange rhythmic fashion, held me back.

By now I was sure that it was Art and equally sure that he must be dead or severely injured at least. He could not have survived a fall into these rocks. The little girl, Nirwana, pulled at my arm to bring me back .

"Alive", she said.

"Alive! How can he be?"

"In water, not on rock. We go down. Come, come, come.

She pointed to one side where Jack had already scrambled over a sharp piece of rock where only his head was visible. That quickly went out of sight, and as we came to a sort of track he called back up to us from further down:

"He's there."

It took us a little while to follow Jack who we found laughing as he sat on a rock. He held out his hand.

It was white.

"Clay, it's clay. It's been daubed all over him but has now been all washed off by the water."

"But where is Art?"

"This wasn't Art. He has already been through the ceremony. This wasn't Art. He is quite safe."

One of the women scowled at Jack. He spoke to her but she shook her head firmly and pointed back up the cliff.

"We are to go back and wait again as the ceremony has been spoiled."

"What ceremony?"

"Its part of the process of becoming a man. The men camp in the valley and initiate the boys. Each one has to jump into the river by turn. It's not dangerous. As they go into the water covered in clay it washes off and they emerge into their new state of manhood. As I said Art has already been through the ceremony. Tomorrow there will be a big dance, a corroboree, and all the new men will participate. That's the one that we have already heard about. We can join in that, but must go back for now.

I thought about the shot that we had heard.

"Who was doing the shooting Jack?"

He stopped smiling.

"That is something that I have to deal with. Do you think that you could manage to divert these men for a moment? I need to speak to your little interpreter."

For an answer I fainted, or rather pretended to. The women all crowded round and made a great fuss. To be honest I had gone through so much in the last few hours that I hardly had to pretend. The two men pushed the women aside.

"Right. You've seen your lad. Now we need to go along with these black bastards."

Jack pushed in beside them.

"Olivia. Are you alright?"

I nodded and lifted my eyebrows in silent question. He gave a slight nod, so I stood up and said that I was recovered.

Chapter 13

The corroboree was under way. I had still not seen Art but I was assured that in time he would appear along with all the newly made men. In the meantime lines of dancers stamped their feet and waved their arms in time to rhythms that were being made on a number of primitive instruments. Some long wooden hollow pieces of wood were adding to the noise. They were blown by some men looking and sounding, for all the world, as if they were real musical instruments.

There was an air of excitement, of anticipation. I felt caught up in the general feeling. Jack was nowhere to be seen. He had started watching with me, then said something to me that I failed to catch as the noise level was so acute. He mouthed something to me and drew back into the darkness.

The whole group were moving together in time to the drumming and the sound of those strange long pipes that they blew into to make a continuous sonorous noise. I have to call it noise. I suppose to them it was a sort of music, but to me it still remained just noise. In time it became so repetitive that I almost fell asleep.

To keep myself awake I tried to look much harder at the ceremony. I thought that I must remember this to tell Pip when we get home. Across from where we were sitting as visitors, I could see the men who were not dancing. Some stood with the firelight playing on them and the enormous old dead tree that was behind them. In the far distance I could just about make out what were either clouds or mountains. It was getting darker and soon the only light would be that provided by the fire. As they danced the dust flew up.

The noise reached a peak then stopped as a line of boys came into view. All were adorned with clay, bits of feathers and a variety of things that were pushed into their hair.   I recognised Art immediately and would have moved to him except that the women to one side of me shook their heads and held onto me. They too chanted and moved their feet in time to the chanting. Unwillingly I stayed in line and kept step. The chanting and dancing went on and on.

One of the women looked familiar and when I looked more closely I could see that it was Mrs Dujane. She smiled at me but shook her head when I opened my mouth to say something. Jack, who had joined us, opened his hand slightly and I saw that he held something in it. I could not determine what it was but when he threw it into the fire there was a tremendous flash of light.

I fell on my knees only to find Walloomba behind me pulling my arm saying:

"Quick, come. Come now."

I turned round to find that he was with Art who clutched my hand and dragged me away from the light. Together we stumbled away into the darkness where Jack was waiting. He had our things that he had somehow gathered together and had his bag. There were gunshots. The natives were screaming now and I couldn't see anything of the two men.

I can hardly remember how we made our escape; it was dark and that helped. We were desperate too so we pushed on tirelessly. I only know that after that first night, as soon as it became dark we stopped, for it was far too dangerous to travel by night. A fall could result in a broken limb so easily

Art was the problem. The ceremony and dance had tired him. He was exhausted. He hadn't the stamina so we carried him, slung between poles that had been thrust though the arms of Jack's jacket to make a crude stretcher, travelling over broken ground that slowed us down considerably. Clambering over the rocks was tiring, and when we stopped we fell asleep almost as soon as we lay down.

It was Art shaking my shoulder that woke me.

"Ma. Wake up."

It took me a little while to do so as I was still so tired from the previous days' exertions. Across the small clearing where we had spent the night I could see that Jack and Walloomba were huddled under their little gunyah that we had found. I wondered why I could see them so clearly in the night. It was a strange light that enabled me to see them. Not the usual emerging dawn and then sudden brightness, but a red glare that was accompanied by a hot bitter smell.

I was about to wake up Jack when Walloomba sat up suddenly completely alert, his eyes gleaming. He threw out a hand sideways hitting jack who groaned:

"Go away."

He hit him again, this time much harder. I heard the thump and I also heard another sound. It was a mixture of drumming and roaring. In my half asleep state I imagined a lion. I shook myself. There were no lions in Australia. I did not imagine the wallaby that now bounded across the clearing. Nor the other animals. Jack was fully awake by now and was grabbing together all our possessions.

"What is it? What is happening?"

Walloomba caught Art by the arm and pushed me before him.

"Run. Run."

The sound was louder now a continuous roar like never ending surf on a shore. Jack followed us urging us on. I followed Art and Walloomba.

"Down here."

I paused. The cleft in the rock looked dark by contrast to the increasing red light. Jack pushed and Walloomba pulled, so I was forced into what turned out to be a deep gully.

"Lie down."

I lay down next to Art who was trembling. I was shaking too. The roaring reached a peak then died away. I went to get up.

"No stay. Wait. We are safe here. It's probably gone now."

I remembered Ma telling me about the time when our shop was burned out. I had gone round there and seen the damage that fire can do. The smell now was similar, hot and bitter. We had to wait until the afternoon before we were able to climb out of our rocky refuge, and it was only because there was a shower of rain that damped everything down that we could do so. We found that the wind had shifted at the last minute by passing our outcrop and so saving us. It had completely changed the look of everything around about, and had destroyed the area where we had camped.

We searched around, for in our rush to escape, we had managed to lose some of our possessions. They had all been consumed, only ash remaining. We took stock of what we had. Walloomba had his bag, of course. I still had a few things and so did Jack, but Art was left with practically nothing.

It was so ironic. When we rescued Art I had carefully made him put on his normal clothes. Now apart from his drawers that he had been sleeping in, everything else was gone. He took these off and put on the little bark loincloth that he had worn in the corroboree. With the white of the ash and the black of the charcoal on his body he looked once again as he had before.

"You had better keep these. I don't seem to be very good at looking after my clothes."

Both Jack and Walloomba laughed.

Walloomba showed Jack a little stone snake that he took out of his bag, and said that it was protecting us. He said that was why we had survived the fire. Jack simply waved the whole idea aside. I ventured that it was Walloomba's version of a guardian angel. This got even less regard from Jack who is, I am coming to see, a much more complicated person than I took him for. He obviously must believe in something. Actually, the longer we are together the more he reveals of himself, and it is difficult not to like him, despite his stubbornness.

With so much less to carry we were our way once again at a much increased speed. My main worry was that we would not be able to find our boat. Jack told me later that his main concern was that it would be gone or damaged. He was quite clear in his mind where it was to be found. In any case Walloomba could be relied upon to find it. It was his country. What irony that Jack had to concede that!

It was exactly where we had left it, but was brimful of rainwater that came in very useful as you might imagine. When we had slaked our thirst and filled our water containers I was about to try to bail out the remainder of the water when Jack stopped me. He and Walloomba simply levered it sideways with a long piece of driftwood. The boat rocked backwards and forwards until there was a great gush of water; and all the bits of twigs and leaves that had fallen to the bottom of the boat came gushing out too. Jack said something about Archimedes that I didn't quite catch. I thought to myself that I would have to ask him about that later, but I never did.

The paddles were nowhere to be seen so we had to make do with poles that we prised loose from the smashed up piles of debris that had been carried down stream. We thought that as we were going down river we could assume that the stream would provide all the power that we needed, and that all we had to do was use the poles to keep us in the centre of the river. Art was laid in the middle of the boat with Jack's coat now providing shelter from a blistering sun. I scooped up some mud and plastered it on me. It soon dried but it was an effective sunscreen and prevented the mosquitoes from getting at me.

And so we floated down the river in some style. I was becoming more hopeful as every mile of bank slid by. Art was not so ill now, and was able share my interest in the scenery. I pointed out to him the creatures that we saw. The birds, of course, were everywhere. Their bright colours were in such contrast to the trees that they showed up dramatically. How strange I thought that such a short way away from here, whole sections of the bush had been taken out by the fire, and yet here, on both sides of the river the trees remained untouched. As I drew Art's attention to each new creature that I spotted, he told me the native name for it, adding each time whether it was good to eat or not.

Both Walloomba and Jack were able to keep us from snagging on fallen trees and were also able to push us away from rocks. Eventually the river opened out so far that we could scarcely see the banks. Then quite abruptly it narrowed forcing us through a fast running stretch that was narrow because of the rocky nature of the landscape, before spewing us out into the sea. I was afraid that we would capsize as the area of sea where we had come out was so very turbulent. The muddy brown river fought against the clear sea water causing whirlpools to form that threatened our safety.

Now Walloomba and Jack had to fight to turn our boat around in order to make it point towards the shore. Once they had done so the breakers pushed us in, driving us towards a fine beach of sparkling coarse sand. At one end of it there was a curious mound of something that attracted my attention and distracted me sufficiently to make me lose my fear of the speed that we were now rushing up the beach.

We hit the sand and I lost my footing and fell over into the water screaming as the salt water stung my scratches and insect bites. Art, with more presence of mind than me, held on until we hit and then jumped clear shouting as he did so, but his shout was to draw our attention to some men who had come out of the undergrowth and run down to the edge of the water carrying spears.

We all stood up to our ankles for a moment before running forward to avoid the next breaker that threatened to overwhelm us and suck us back. The thin black totally naked men looked at us. I sensed that they were as frightened of us as I certainly was of them.

Chapter 14

It was Walloomba who broke the silence. He spoke in a strange dialect and enunciated each word harshly as if commanding them. They ignored him. Instead they watched me and I thought that they have probably seen so few white women in their lives that I must have been a complete novelty. If they had seen any they would certainly have been wearing more than I had on at the moment. If I had to describe my apparel, only one word would suffice: indecorous. The way that the men looked at me soon persuaded me that they were in no fashion afraid, but were simply curious.

I put my arm around Art, conscious that, apart from a very torn shift and an extremely ragged skirt, which I might add was missing the hem for I had torn it off at sometime either to bind up a cut or for some other equally utilitarian purpose, I had never worn so little in my life. It's true that I still had on my boots. Fear of snakes had made me cling to them, despite Art, Jack and Walloomba assuring me that they would more fearful of me.

I had always protected myself from the ravages of the fierce Australian sun. In contrast to my Ma whose poor face was so scarred that more sun did it no harm at all mine was pearly white and flawless when I was young. I had always prided myself on my pale skin, that many a lady would have envied, despite the fact that I never hid my convict mother origins. Now, I had certainly lost that pale and interesting look that I had shared with Estella. My arms were closer in hue to those of Lizbeth whose duskiness was owed to her mother who came not from England or Ireland but somewhere south of Sydney, according to Ma.

So now here I was, reduced by the sun, and layers of dirt to what imagined a gypsy woman looked like in Ireland. All thought of my skin colour and apparel disappeared as Walloomba spoke again sharply emphasising his words with quick chopping gestures. Again they ignored him, preferring to gaze upon me as the latest interesting person who had come into their lives. Later I was to learn that what fascinated them was the fact that I was half white and half brown.

Walloomba slowly opened his bag and drew out the stone serpent and pointed it at them. I had heard tell of the way some black people could point at others and that the effect was to take away their will to live. Was I witnessing this now? The men backed away. They seemed to be in awe of the snake. They turned and ran back into the bush.

In the most matter of fact way possible Walloomba turned to us and said:

"Gather some wood we need to make a fire."

I thought that he meant that we needed to dry our clothes. I had learned in the short while that we had been together that if Walloomba said we should do something then it was best to do it. While Jack hauled the boat up, using the surf to help him, Art and I gathered driftwood. Once again I marvelled at the ease with which Walloomba twirled a stick and produced a glowing ember that he blew into a blaze. Our fire was going well when Art, who was opposite me and looking into the bush, opened his eyes wide and whispered:

"They're back."

Chapter 15

When I turned round, I saw that they were indeed back, this time in force, and were laden with spears, clubs and throwing sticks. Behind them a gaggle of women and children followed. They too were laden and as they pressed closer I smelled their rankness. The women had all put something on their hair to keep off the insects. Whatever it was, and however efficacious it was, it certainly smelt vile. What they were carrying did not however. It was food, meat that needed to be cooked and that was why Walloomba had demanded from us the driftwood just as he had demanded meat from this tribe.

We set to cooking the meat that seemed to be a haunch of some large animal that Jack and Walloomba dealt with by spearing it and roasting it. Again the driftwood came into play to make a spit so that the haunch could be turned regularly to prevent it burning. I must confess my belly rumbled as loudly as the others' did and I was hard put to wait until the meat was properly cooked. As it cooked Walloomba harangued the crowd of blacks who listened carefully, then regretfully departed, looking back at me. I gathered from Walloomba as we ate our meal that he had persuaded them that I was a sort of minor deity!

The curious mound that had attracted my attention turned out to be a pile of empty shells, something that pleased Walloomba. He told me, as we waited for the meat to cook, that the shells were the remains of shellfish that the natives had taken from the sea. He said that this meant that we could not only get fish, but shellfish to supplement our diet.

After our meal Jack, Walloomba and Art set out to go fishing. Art was much improved in his health. Resting in the boat and now eating a nourishing meal had been just what he had needed. I smiled at the way that he joined Walloomba and Jack quite naturally and thought all too soon he would no longer be my little lad.

While Jack and Walloomba looked after Art I walked along the beach seeking some privacy until I came to the edge of the river as it ran into the sea. There I removed my torn clothing and waded into the river to wash all the sweat and mud off my body. I looked at it. It was certainly the very first time that I had ever seen myself with no clothes on at all in the open air. Somehow my insect bites had disappeared. I marvelled at how brown my hands and arms were in total contrast to the rest of my body that remained white with the blue veins accentuating the pale hue of my skin. I had long since lost my hat and I wondered whether my face was also as tanned as my arms. I pushed my nose to one side to try to see how brown it had become. A still pool of water gave me a proper opportunity to examine my face.

It was certainly Olivia Gargery who looked back at me, but a very changed Olivia. I reflected that I was also quite changed in other ways too. I washed my clothes that were stiff with salt and mud. They were still stained when I had finished, but once I had hung them on some stunted bushes they soon began to dry in the breeze and I knew they would be more comfortable.

Some birds flew up catching my attention and as they did so I imagined that I saw Jack. But when I looked more closely I thought that I must have been mistaken. I wondered idly what I would have done had it been him. Would I have snatched up my clothes in maidenly modesty? I think not. We had shared too much for that sort of behaviour on my part. The thought shocked me. It was a delicious shock though, and as it was never going to happen, I indulged myself as a femme fatale. I thought of Lola Montez and began to understand something of how and why she had behaved as she did.

I became aware of the strength of the sun for I felt my back prickling as its rays struck it so I sat upon a flat rock in the shade of my drying clothes. I should have felt worried about what faced us in trying to return home. We had been swept down to the coast where any chance of getting back up the river in our little boat was negligible. Instead I felt a great pervasive calmness; a calm that came with knowing that Jack and Walloomba had rescued Art and got us away safely. All I had to do now was continue to trust them to finish the job. As I thought this I stood up and caught sight of something that I had missed before. It was some wreckage from a boat and it included several barrels, none of which had anything in them.

I dressed myself and, feeling somewhat cleaner, I picked up my boots and made my way back through the hot sand to my companions. They had not wasted time in cleaning themselves, preferring to join the black men who had come back, in another fishing expedition that had proved to be so successful that we soon had another meal; this time of grilled fish and some sort of greens that the blackfellas gathered for us. We were making up for all those skimpy meals of oatmeal that had sustained us so far.

Following the meal I told the others what I had found. They followed me back to where I had seen the wreckage. Jack was cock-o-hoop over my discovery.

"You know what this means? We can use the barrel staves to make paddles."

So they set to work shaping the staves that they broke away from one of the barrels. Soon he had shaped two paddles and John put the other two barrels into the river tied with vine to prevent them from drifting away.

"If we soak them the wood will swell and we can fill them with water. We are going to need water if we go to sea."

"Go to sea? Why should we do that?"

"Olivia, It's the only way that we can get back to Sydney. We must put out to sea and either be spotted by a passing ship, or sail down the coast southwards until we reach Sydney Heads and turn into the harbour."

"It sounds perilous."

"Not as perilous as staying here. Sooner or later they are going to catch up with us. They think that we still have the papers that prove that John Adam does not own the land. I'm sure that they will not stop until they get them back."

"But we don't have the papers."

"We know that, but *they* don't. So come on we have work to do."

For the next day we prepared for our journey. Art and Walloomba caught more fish and I helped to smoke them. We did it over a fire that Walloomba magically kindled by twirling a stick until the friction caused enough heat to ignite some kindling. By now Art had given up any idea of wearing clothes and went around as naked as Walloomba. Strangely I was unaffected by this. I wore the absolute minimum, and the clothes that I kept on, a shift and boots were more related to being functional than preserving my modesty. The truth was, I was more concerned to get home than to keep up any standards. It did cross my mind however that if we did sail round the heads and into Sydney harbour I ought to do something to make myself look presentable.

I said as much to Jack who hooted with laughter. Then seeing that he had offended me, asked my pardon and promised to give it some thought. He did his best with what he manage to acquire from the black women, but as their standard of dress left much to be desired in terms of European fashion, I thanked Jack politely and stowed what he had gathered in the stern, as I had learned to call it, of the boat.

Jack also mended several other barrels that he lashed into the boat, saying that they would make the boat more buoyant. Finally he constructed what he called an outrigger which he again insisted would make our boat much safer in the rougher seas that we faced when we ventured out beyond the shore.

Walloomba had woven together some stiff leaves into the semblance of a small sail that he now fixed to a post in the middle of the boat. I thought that it looked terribly flimsy and made the mistake of saying so. Walloomba went off in a huff. Jack assured me that because it was so small it would help us along but not get us into any trouble if it blew hard out to sea.

I wanted to know why we could not stay near the shore as we went south. His answer was that it would be too dangerous.

"We must be far enough out to sea to avoid being driven inshore onto the rocks."

By now I was beginning to lose my calmness. I wanted to know whether this was going to work.

"Just remember the Bryants. They were convicts. They stole a boat in Sydney during the night in March 1791. It was actually the Governor's own boat, a cutter. They had other escapees with them, and they sailed from Sydney right up the coast to the Dutch East Indies. They survived the journey and would have got clean away had they not quarrelled amongst themselves."

Art hung on Jack's every word, drinking in the narrative in such a way that I became concerned. I said lightly to him that it would be splendid to be home soon with his father. he agreed without any enthusiasm.

At last we were ready to leave. We dragged the boat into the sea, pushed it through the surf that swept around us, and using our new paddles we managed to move out almost to where a huge head of rock stuck out. We could see the brown stain of the river as it flowed into the sea. John pointed out that the river had slowed down considerably since our arrival. He said that the rains had stopped and the flooding had gone down, so if we were still being pursued it would be easier for them now.

Our tiny craft began to move up and down in the swell which made me nervous. Then to my relief, once the sail had been pulled up by Walloomba, we began to move, and the up and down motion lessened somewhat. John looked anxiously at the shore where we had made our fire and smoked the fish. The sea birds that had screamed and fought over the guts of the fish that we threw onto the sand had long since departed.

Instead we heard shouts. There on the strand were tiny figures that we could see were white men. As we watched a puff of smoke came from one of them who was kneeling down. A second or two later it was followed by a curious buzzing sound above our heads.

"Oh! Bloody hell and deepest damnation", said John.

"Quick. Paddle. Paddle like hell."

"What"…,I began only to stop when I saw another puff of smoke and then a little splash on the sea between us and the shore.

Art said:

"It's guns, they are shooting at us. There, can you see? There they go again. See the smoke?"

Glancing sideways I saw two puffs of smoke that erupted simultaneously then drifted away more rapidly than the first ones. This time there was no whining, buzzing noise, nor any splash.

"Aha! Shouted Jack. They forgot to aim off for the wind. Keep paddling and we shall beat them yet."

The wind had indeed sprung up. I stopped looking at the shore and turned to the front only to shriek in terror. We were bearing down on a huge black cliff, a great wall of rock.

Chapter 16

"Stop, stop", I wailed, but Walloomba and Jack ignored me, laughing at my terror.

The next second we ran straight into a wall, a wall of rain! Rain that was so dense that it was almost like being underwater. Now we began to wallow as we lost way for the boat was quickly filling with rainwater Both Walloomba and Jack began desperately to throw the water over the side using their hands . Art and I joined in.

Abruptly the rain ceased. We had sailed through a tropical cloudburst and were now back out in the usual hot sunlight. We struggled on and as we did so everything began to steam. I fished up the shells that we had kept for eating and we used them to throw the water out. Soon only a few inches were left. Discarding my last shreds of modesty, I took off my shift leaving a sufficiency of undergarments to preserve some decency and used it to mop up the last of the water, squeezing it out just as my mother made me do when I helped her do the washing. What would she say if she could see me now?

"Needs must when the devil drives". I said to Jack who looked at me woodenly.

The sun and the rain continued the process of drying, and as we moved along I asked Jack why we seemed to be moving so slowly. He explained that it was because we were a little ways out from the shore. In fact were doing very comfortably. He instructed Art to keep his eye on a particular rock and sure enough Art said it seemed to be moving steadily back from us. Of course it was really we who were moving in the opposite direction. I asked Jack how he thought we were doing.

"I am glad we got away when we did. My worry now is the night. We have no compass. I think that sailing in the dark will be dangerous, but then so will trying to land be equally so."

Walloomba laughed. He was at the back of the boat holding onto the piece of vine that he had twisted into a rope to hold our poor apology for a sail. Next to him sat Art who was assisting John to hold a piece of carved barrel as a sort of rudder. W laughed again till the tears ran down his cheeks. We all looked at him. Had he gone mad?

"You white men. You are so very clever. Why do you think the great serpent put the stars up in the sky? How do you think we ignorant heathens have been moving around in this land if we do not use the stars and the moon? Maybe we don't have all those things that you hold in your hand that help you. Maybe we can't read those things that you call books. Maybe we are poor ignorant savages who lack all the advantages of your so-called civilisation. But look what you do to your own people. You tear them away from their homeland. You punish them. You hang them."

He stopped. We all fell silent and only the continuous slap of the salt water waves against the boat was heard until Jack said tentatively:

"So, you think we should sail at night?"

"No, it's too dangerous."

Jack looked angry. I could see that he was about to say something that we all might regret so I asked Walloomba what he meant. He explained that we could sail by night or we could land; both options were dangerous, but the least dangerous was probably to land. I asked him what tribe he came from, mainly to fill the uneasy gap that now existed. He replied that he regarded himself as coming from no particular tribe ever since he had come under the influence of grog.

"It fills my soul and transports me to the edge of dreamtime where I feel I should be, not in this unreal copy of that world. The other reason that I claim no membership of any particular tribe is that I have travelled around. Jack will tell you that I have moved all over the land as much as he has. Just as he has used his tools, I have drawn on tribal knowledge; all tribal knowledge, for no tribe has all the answers.

Jack sneered. He wanted to know just what sort of knowledge Walloomba had that was useful.

"I brought Yellow Alice to you."

That made Jack thoughtful, for he remembered as I did, that Alice had claimed more than just being in touch with Walloomba.

Again we sat silent listening to the slap, slap of the waves as we moved gradually homewards.

"But all those stories that you tell, the explanations for the sun's rising and the great Emu in the sky and the other things. They aren't true are they? They can't be true can they?"

To my surprise Walloomba looked sharply at Art who had posed the question and said:

"No. But it does not matter. We all need stories to help us to understand our world and to help us to deal with the many problems that we face as we make our way through it. Listen and I will tell you some of these stories. It doesn't matter which tribe tells them, or whether they are true or not.

Every night the sun goes to bed. She is tired for she has had to cross the sky holding up a bright light for people to see by. When she is rested, she gets up and paints herself, just as I have seen white women paint themselves, She uses ground red rock. She spills it as she makes herself ready. You have seen me make fire from nothing; now she does that too and makes a lit branch to carry all day. The paint that she spills colours the sky. We know that when we see that glow that she is coming, so we celebrate her coming each day.

Her sister is the moon. She too journeys across the sky but she gets weaker and weaker as she finds nothing to eat until there is nothing left of her. That is when her sister, the sun, takes pity on her and feeds her until she begins to grow once more. When she is full her sister becomes tired of having to care for her and stops feeding her so that she grows thin once more."

"Those are lovely stories", I said. "But they are just stories, myths."

"Yes, they are", answered Walloomba, but went on:

"Now, would you like to tell us the story of how all the animals in the world were put into one boat to save them from drowning. Or perhaps you would like to tell us how your god put a rainbow in the sky as a promise."

I opened my mouth to say something when Jack forestalled me by saying harshly:

"It won't do you know. It won't do at all. I threw away my Bible but there's some what need it, or something like it. We all need something more in our lives, something that makes sense of life. We must be here for some reason. Pretty stories that children and simple folk enjoy are not enough."

I sat amazed at his outburst. We sat in silence.

"Perhaps, Art ventured, "Perhaps it would be best if we stopped talking about any of this until we are safely home."

Wallambollo nodded approvingly and Jack smiled. I thought how strange it was that Art got on so well with Jack and Walloomba, but was nowhere as easy with his own father. This made me think of Pip. He must be wondering what on earth had happened to us. At least he was safely at home and would be there to welcome us when we arrived. I came out of my daydream of home and looked at the three men who would get me there. I thought that even Gulliver wanted to get home from his travels. I nearly said as much to Jack, but I stopped as I realised that for all his education as a geologist, he knew nothing at all about literature.

So by common agreement we dropped our discussion, and I could see that this pleased Art who busied himself with assisting Walloomba to steer the boat. He took over the paddle that acted as our rudder while Walloomba used dry leaves that he had brought along, making them into crude hats. We all gratefully put them on, mindful of the effect that the sun's rays bouncing off the waves would be having on us.

Chapter 17

I knew from that time when we went by boat to the Clontarf picnic that even a short sojourn upon the waters can result in damaging effects. On that occasion several ladies ignored all warnings and removed their bonnets and then failed to use their parasols, seduced by the sea breeze that blew about them into thinking that the sun was not that strong. Luckily they had marquees for all when we arrived, and so they were able to rest in the shade, but some had blinding headaches. My Ma failed to find a saying that was appropriate, which surprised me; instead she simply muttered: 'Silly bitches!'

Now with the weather so much improved we sailed along calmly. Walloomba had constructed a primitive line and from a sea teeming with fish he managed to catch some. I persuaded Jack to run our boat ashore as the seas were so calm, for I knew that we ought to take any and every opportunity to have some meals other than the dried fish that we had smoked and brought with us. I was sure that we would be sure to find some vegetables. So he turned and we headed into a tiny bay where we gathered some edible plants that Walloomba said were safe to eat. These went well with our freshly caught fish. I sat at ease afterwards while Walloomba and Art went together to see whether they could find some fresh water.

I must have dozed off. Jack coughed and when I looked in his direction I could see that he was uneasy. He began to say something then stopped. I waited. He fidgeted and avoided looking at me. It was just as if…

Before I could finish my thought he said:

"Olivia, when we reach Sydney. When we get home, that is, I expect I shall not see you again."

I knew then that I had to stop him before he said something that would destroy my peace.

"Tell me more about those escaped convicts. Did they get clean away? They were Brians I believe you said. Were they married?"

"Bryants; they were a Mr William and Mrs Mary Bryant. Yes they were wed. Once they reached Timor they told the Governor there that they were survivors, having been shipwrecked. Amazingly, he believed them. He looked after them and the whole party waited for a ship to take them back to England. They could have got clean away if William had kept his mouth shut. No one knows why, but William Bryant got drunk and told the truth to the Governor. The truth. It's hard not to tell people what's on your mind you know."

I ignored his last comment. I looked out to sea.

"What happened then?"

"They were all chained up in irons, and soon after that William and his son died. Some of the others died too while they were being shipped back to England, but Mary survived. Rather sadly her daughter died on the voyage back. Then somehow the newspapers got hold of the story; they love a sad tale like that. Lots of folks got interested and the upshot was that she got a pardon and stayed in England."

"So she lost everyone, but survived."

"Yes she did. Olivia..." he began, but did not go on as Walloomba and Art came whooping back carrying a full barrel of fresh water.

Jack smiled regretfully at me. I had seen that look in so many men's faces in my time not to know the sort of feelings that was behind it. In the past it had meant nothing, nothing at all, but now I was afraid; and it was my feelings that made me fearful.

Chapter 18

At first their whoops of glee were because they had found fresh water, then they became more excited as they saw out almost on the horizon a ship. Jack and I had been too preoccupied with other matters to have looked at the sea otherwise we might have spotted it earlier. Now we all got excited. Not stopping to put anything into our boat, we pushed it across the accumulated shells and seaweed and launched it. The smell of the crushed seaweed stays with me still. When I look back to that moment I realise that it was the time when everything changed for me. Nothing was ever the same after that moment. I moved from being a young woman to being middle aged and staid. I had to do it in order to preserve myself and everything that I thought was important.

We shouted. We waved. The ship ploughed on regardless, until all we could see was its stern and the smoke drifting back from its funnel. We stopped our puny efforts at attracting the sea monster and sat dejected. Our boat now began to be caught by the waves that the ship had made in passing us. We dipped up and down, and at the summit of one of those waves we all saw that the ship was changing shape. From being a small object that had been getting smaller, it started to elongate until we saw it side on.

"It's turning around", said Art.

It was indeed and soon we saw its bows pointed back towards our little boat as it grew larger and more distinct. Now we could see men and women crowded at the front. I learned later that bets were being taken by some of the men on how many of us we were in the boat. Others on how long it would take to get to us.

The ship, an impossibly clean and polished thing, slowed as it reached us. A sparkling gangway, all mahogany and brass, was lowered and an immaculately dressed young officer came down it to assist me to go up to the deck. Behind me Art was helped by Jack to follow me into the midst of a chattering crowd of men and women. Walloomba was left to fend for himself. They almost cast him adrift with the boat as they assumed that he had merely brought us out to the ship. There were many disapproving looks from the crowd when I insisted that he should accompany us.

I felt intensely aware that I was to all these well-dressed ladies and gentlemen half-naked. Walloomba was practically so, and was discreetly hurried to another part of the ship. A sheet was found for me, and another for Art. No one thought to cover Jack's torso that remained bare and tanned and handsome, and was subject to curious and, dare I say it, admiring glances from several young women. I felt outrage. Not at the way that they had treated Walloomba, but at way that Jack was being ogled. I had to admit it to myself as I was led below to the unbelievable luxury of a bath in hot water, courtesy of Captain Aveburry, that I was jealous and felt possessive.

Art was soon dressed in clothes borrowed from a young lad, whilst I had the pick of a dozen outfits that were offered to me by those very same young women who had aroused my ire at their interest in Jack. I warned Art to say nothing. I said that it was important, for reasons that I would explain when we got home, for him to leave me to tell everyone what had happened.

Ma would have been proud of me at last as that evening I told my story in a carefully modulated ladylike voice to an eager crowd, whose attention I had in full as I outlined how Art and I had been rescued by my saviour Jack. I looked toward him where he stood silent and handsome as I explained our good fortune in having such a noted geologist as he to come to our aid. I took some questions about how I had suffered and what I had done to mitigate those sufferings. To questions as to why I was roaming around in the outback with my son, I gave vague answers until both Jack and the captain declared that I had done enough to satisfy their curiosity and that I should now be allowed to rest.

For the remainder of the time that we were in the ship I kept to my cabin. I thought that the less that we said the better. Jack spoke to me briefly and he agreed with me that we should keep our explanations to a minimum. He obviously wished to speak more with me, but I was never alone for a sufficiency of time for us to have a sustained conversation

I had forgotten however how persistent the gentlemen of the press could be, and Jack had to manufacture a story for them when they came aboard at Sydney. It was a story that they largely ignored, as they preferred to publish one that would interest their readers more that the prosaic one that he told them.

I still have the newspaper cutting for Elaine Pomeroy cut it out of the newspaper for me.

Flood Victims Dramatic Rescue

A few days ago, flood victims, Mrs Olivia Gargerry, Mr. Jack King and Master Arthur Gargerry, were snatched to safely from a boiling sea when their frail craft was spotted by the Ocean Star steamship. Thanks to an alert crew member they were plucked to safety moments before it sank, never to be seen again. Captain Aveburry of the Ocean Star said modestly that he had just been in the right place at the right time. Some would see the hand of the Almighty in this, he added.

All three were suffering from exposure and excessive sunburn. They had been overwhelmed when their small boat had been swept out to sea by the excessive floods inland caused by the torrential rain. Native tribes had pursued them, but they had escaped.

Jack King, who is a geologist, had been prospecting for minerals that might be useful to this country in future. He had previously rescued Mrs Gargerry, who with her son had been exploring the outback with a view to writing a book about the aborigines and their quaint customs who live there.

Turn to page 6 for further details

It just shows how you can never really believe what you read in the papers

Chapter 19

At Sydney we hurried ashore. Jack got a cab and we all piled into it. I was anxious to get home to see Pip. Art seemed less keen. I think that having been the main character in what was to him simply an adventure, he would have liked it to continue. He had also got quite attached to Walloomba and Jack in a fashion that was totally unlike the way he related to his father. This bothered me, but I reasoned that once we were all home again everything would settle down. Before we reached the shop Jack had the cab stop and said that he would join us later.

I felt guilty at him simply going off in this fashion. I thought that I ought to say something for I guessed that once I saw Phillip I might not be able to say anything.

"Jack", I said, "About my book."

He looked at me. The look that he gave me chilled me. The horse snorted and the cab moved and the cabbie said:

"Do you want to go on?"

Jack ignored him. I had only wanted to mention the book as a way in to say how foolish I had been. I only wished to apologise when Jack burst out with:

"My Good God Olivia! What is it about that book? Look, I'm sorry that it got burned in the fire, but it was just a book wasn't it?

Stung into a reply I said that no book was just 'a book'. I could see from the way that his face set as I said this that I ought to stop, but I just couldn't help myself.

"Through thousands of years books have contained knowledge and stories that can be transferred to anyone minded to read them."

The cabbie said wearily;

"I can't wait all day."

In my eagerness to explain how nothing would, ever, ever, replace books, I seized Jack's arm. He drew it away coldly.

" I think that you care more for your books than any person."

He said this in such a sad slow way that I was moved as never before.

"Drive on", he called to an increasingly impatient cabbie.

"Not so!" I called after him.

"I care for Phillip and Art"

Then when he was nearly gone I whispered:

"And you."

I turned wiping my eyes that had got dust in them so making them water, or so I explained to Lizbeth who just then came out of the shop.

Lizbeth greeted us by asking after my brother, and I just remembered in time that we were supposed to have been in Perth. I said that he was well. I thought that in due course I should have to tell Lizbeth the whole story. Just now though I wanted to see Phillip. We went in and sat down.

I would have gone looking for him had not Mrs Dujane not come walking through the door as if she had just been out for a stroll in Sydney and had decided to drop into our shop to look at the latest novel. She was thinner than she had been formerly, but apart from that was, exactly as I remembered her at the Corroboree.

Lizbeth gave her strange look before going back into the shop. When Alice went, she was insistent that I call her Alice now that I knew her history, Lizbeth came back to talk to me. She wanted to know what Mrs Dujane had wanted. Before I could tell her she burst out that she was trying to ruin her. I was quite taken aback.

"Who is trying to ruin you?"

"That Mrs Dujane. She insists that we are sisters. Not real sisters but sisters who share the same background. She says that I am not to be ashamed of being half native like her. That woman. She thinks that as she is a bastard and half aborigine, anyone else like her wishes the whole world to be aware of the fact."

"But", I began, then stopped.

I vaguely knew that Lizbeth's origins were tangled up in some way with her mother being a native of Australia, but I had never thought anything of it. When Phillip had come to Australia he had taken us for sisters, not because we were like each other, but because we were both employed in the bookshop. Of course she was as dark as I was fair, but no one ever talked about it.

I had been brought up alongside Lizbeth who was almost an older sister to me. Her real name was Elizabeth Wright but I never ever remember anyone calling her that except Toby Davis on that occasion just before he died. He was also employed in our shop, and swindled Ma out of it; but that is another story entirely.

Lizbeth never minded being called Lizbeth, but drew the line at Liz. She used to joke that she would never marry a lord, which was her ambition, if she was called Liz. When we worked together in Ma's shop she attracted men like Ma's home-made jam attracted flies. Slim with enough voluptuousness to overcome her simple clothing that she wore, she was, with her long dark rope of hair and long eyelashes a favourite with men customers. She would charm them, and Toby would take their orders. When she did marry it was not to a lord, but a dull stick of a fellow who brought in a regular wage. My mother used to say of him: 'handsome is as handsome does.'

I once heard myself being described as a piece of porcelain, pale and perfect. I avoided the sun so was as pale as Lizbeth was dark. She never minded it and despite any amount of exposure to its rays, she never seemed to get any darker. I suppose we all avoided the truth: Lizbeth's mother had been a black native.

I could see how Mrs Dujane would want to use Lizbeth in her fight with the authorities. Her battle with them about the rights of the black people came before anything, and I only knew one thing that she held dearer than that.

"She knows too about your Ma and Mrs Kaye."

That stopped me. I knew that Mrs Kaye had something dark in her past that she had confided to my mother, something so shocking that my mother refused to talk about it.

Mrs Kaye had helped me when Ma began to lose her wits. I had met Mrs Emilie Kaye, to give her full name, when she was employed, even as I was at that time, in the Girl's School at Parramatta. I had to take the job because we lost the shop to Toby when he swindled us, although I never realised that until later on. She was second in charge at the industrial school in Parramatta where they also had an asylum. One day, which had been a particularly difficult one for me, for Ma was either getting forgetful or would go out and accost total strangers, I told Mrs Kaye. It was just after Ma had almost set light to herself. It was only Lizbeth's quick thinking that saved her. Mrs Kaye listened most sympathetically to me, then suggested a home she knew somewhere in Maitland, which meant I would have quite a journey to see her if I put her there, but at least she would have devoted care.

She frightened me by telling me of a woman who had died of burns, which she had suffered from smoking a pipe that she had dropped onto her clothes. I know now that she was using this knowledge to influence my decision. I must say though that, even before hearing this sad story I had quite made up my mind. My Ma had to be looked after.

Lizbeth looked at me. It was a piteous look. I felt for her. It wasn't enough that she had not been able to have children, despite being so good with them, but now this Mrs Dujane was foisting onto Lizbeth her views. I felt very angry. I had no quarrel with Yellow Alice declaiming to the world her origins. After all, I had done the same in respect of my own case, making sure that all knew that I was the daughter of a convict.

In my blind haste to be so correct I neglected to see what pain it gave my Ma, whose only concern was that I should marry well and have a much better life than the one she had experienced. How we hurt people through our desire to do what we want. Now here was Yellow Alice insisting that Lizbeth, who had so wanted to marry a lord, was a bastard and a half caste, which might be true, but it was no one's business except Lizbeth's.

I resolved to act. I drew upon what Estella had said to me when we worked together helping those poor girls who came to Australia from England. I heard again Mrs Chisholm's voice urging me to be the example that these young women lacked. I would act, maybe not precisely in the way that would have pleased Caroline Chisholm, but the end result would be worth it. But first I had to find out more about Mrs Kaye.

"What does she know?"

"She overheard Mrs Kaye telling your Ma something." Your Ma was urging her to tell everything so she poured it out. She did not know that Yellow Alice was listening. It was about the time when Mrs Kaye was a girl in the old country. Seemingly she was sent to prison for a terrible crime. She was in Millbank prison in London for years."

"Did she actually commit this terrible crime?"

"Oh! Yes. She was the one that did it. It caused a terrible stir at the time she said. Then they released her. She went abroad then came to Australia helped by her relatives. It seems that she wanted to clear up any misunderstandings about her crime. She asked your Ma what to do."

"I bet my Ma had some saying to cover the situation!"

"No doubt, no doubt."

"I don't remember much more except a letter was mentioned. Mrs Kaye thought that she ought to write a letter."

I thought carefully. I knew that if my Ma had been told something in confidence that she would never pass it on. Her work with young women who had been so wronged by men meant that ever after she had helped them she often saw them better themselves. With a word she could have ruined them and any happiness that they now had achieved.

I hoped that Mrs Dujane had not told anyone else. I had to get to her and stop her mouth before she did so. This was a time for fighting fire with fire. It was not a time for niceities.

"Did Mrs Dujane tell you where you can reach her?"

"Yes. She expects me to go down to the office that they have set up; you know the one where the Australian Women's Suffrage Society also has an office. What are you going to do?"

"Never you mind. Leave it to me. We do not need to involve anyone else in this. I can deal with it quite satisfactorily. Just go home to that dull dog of a husband that loves you so and do nothing. And, tell no one anything of this matter. No one? Do you understand me?"

Lizbeth looked quite frightened. I must have raised my voice. No doubt she was thinking of the time that she was used as bait to deal with an odious character who subsequently turned up dead in Neutral bay.

"Don't worry. Once I have said what I have to say to Yellow Alice she will leave you well alone I promise."

Lizbeth smiled happily. We had been through a few difficult times together where we had come out none the worse, so she trusted me. She gathered her shawl and bag and went.

Chapter 20

I was saved from having to go to see whether I could find out where Pip had got to for he suddenly made a dramatic entrance. Art ran at him and threw himself into his father's arms much to Pip's amazement and my relief. Jack looked shifty, but when I had told our story including the rescue by boat and all, Pip became all manly and insisted that he shook the hand of his wife's and son's saviour. Jack now looked embarrassed. He would not look at me, and to be honest I could not face him either. I kept repeating under my breath to myself 'nothing happened', though secretly I knew that it could have so easily.

Art became boisterous from too much wine and attention, so we threatened him with packing him off to bed if he did not sit quietly. Pip then told us of the amazing events of his life while I had been away. I do not know and cannot even begin to guess who was the more amazed. I had thought that my story was so full of outlandish detail that it almost impossible to believe it. Now here was Pip spelling out a yarn that almost defied belief.

The next day I went straight away to see Mrs Dujane who pursed her lips and screwed up her face in such a fashion that I knew I was not at all welcome. I was dressed in the clothes that I had been given on the ship, and I think that it is fair to say that the message that I intended to convey by so dressing was not lost on her. Nevertheless she offered me tea that sat in the cups between us cooling as we talked. I say, we talked, but in all honesty I gave her not he slightest chance to say one word. I was all fired up just like a cannon that has been loaded with grapeshot, and I meant to fire and wound and disable my opponent so badly that she would retire from the field immediately.

I told her that I knew that she had come by the mine papers dishonestly, and I further knew with whom she was in league. This last was a lie, but I had a shrewd suspicion that it was true and watching her face I saw my shot had gone home. Now it was time to deliver the coup de grace. I said:

"Mrs Dujane, if you ever say another word to anyone about Lizbeth and her parents I shall take the following course of action: first, I shall lay an information against you that will ensue in you being taken up for felony; next I shall make sure that all those who work for the betterment of black people in Australia shall hear of your larceny; and last of all, if you do not desist from this foolish attempt to recruit Lizbeth in your, no doubt, worthy cause I shall speak to the appropriate authorities who will remove your son from you to be brought up as a white boy. You will never see him again."

She tried to look as if it didn't matter to her, but I knew better. You may think that I was cruel, particularly as there was such a movement to remove boys such as Mrs Dujane's son being considered. It was a threat that I was quite ready to bring about, but equally I thought that her feeling for her son in particular would win out against her feelings for black people in general.

I gathered myself up and swept out. I had used all my ammunition. It was time to let the enemy make an honourable retreat.

The Magwitch Legacy

Phillip's Story

Chapter 1

My life settled down considerably when Livvy found that gold that had been hidden in the china. I must say that I was in a foul mood and bad temper when Pip gave us those ugly china things as a wedding present. I took them home and put them into the attic and forgot all about them. I went out drinking with my mates because I truly thought that my marriage was a sham. A great deal happened after that, but that's all in the past now including my involvement with the Kellys. Sure, I was there and sure, I saw what happened at the end, but by then I was no longer part of it. I was certainly nowhere near when he was hanged.

Livvy is my wife, really Olivia, but everyone who knows her well calls her Livvy. I suppose you could say that I tricked her into marrying me because I knew that she really wanted to train as a nurse. It was after that attempt on the life of Prince Alfred in 1868 when he attended the Sailor's Picnic in Clontarf just outside Sydney. A disaffected Irishman (are there any other sort when you think how Ireland has been treated by the English?) came up behind the Prince and fired a revolver at him. The wound was serious, but fortunately for him, not fatal. He had to spend the next two weeks being looked after by some newly trained nurses who had come out to Australia.

Livvy had been at the picnic because John Adam was there, so she knew all about it; but had she not been at that event she could hardly not have known all the details for there was a mighty public meeting the following day to protest about the outrage. In any case it was all in the papers that whipped up feelings against the Irish. My mother-in-law who had married a James O'Brian, was worried. Would the mob break her shop windows? The only good thing that came out of it was the collection of money to build a new hospital. I think everyone was so ashamed at what had happened they rushed to make amends. They hanged the would-be assassin of course.

That's Australia for you. Flogging and hanging for the lower classes, while the rich get even richer. I was against John Adam even spending good money on the picnic; why, I wanted to know wasn't he spending money on his own workers? I also upset Livvy's Ma when I made dark comments about natural justice and how the nobility would all get their just deserts one day. I never really meant anything by it, but I was to find later that my comments were noted; and it was only because I had come out to Australia of my own free will that nothing was done at that time.

Anyway, Livvy was so struck by the idea of nurses who were trained by the great Florence Nightingale who had made such an impression in the Russian war, that she too wanted to be a nurse. Her mother tried to talk her out of it. She wouldn't listen. She was a stubborn woman then and still is, even more so than I am.

I got her to promise to marry me if they did not select her for nurse training. And because they were such a load of stuck up bastards, they turned her down. Some would say that it was her own fault, for as the daughter of a transported convict her in Australia, Livvy gloried in her lowly past, making no secret of it to the despair of her convict Ma. It put backs up and, although I love her dearly, even I, with all my shouting about the rights of the common man, could see the sense of keeping quiet on this score.

I was a fully qualified blacksmith when I came out to Australia hoping that I would find less corruption and a brotherhood of workers. I was disappointed, of course. I came out looking for a Mr Pip Pirrip who had also started as a blacksmith in England until a certain Abel Magwitch made him a gentleman. I thought that he would be sympathetic to me and my kind, but he was a bigger snob than them all! He tried to turn John Adam, his business partner, into what might pass as a gentleman in Australia and to a certain extent he was successful. John Adam was the driving force in Adam and Pirrip, a firm that John set up by using Pip Pirrip. John did all the real work and Pip used all those connections that he had made when he was taken under the wing of Lady Spens.

I suppose it was having a son of my own that really made me think about my life. Toby's death also contributed to my change of attitude. When he slid off that roof and I had to run away yet again, it made me think, I can tell you.

I was still angry about the way decent working men were treated in the colony, but I now sought other channels for my hot feelings about the injustice of it all. Other men had been transported for combining against injustice; now, here in this new world, they were banding together as brothers in order to protect themselves against greed and money grubbing employers who wanted to grind them down just as they had done in the old country.

In concerning myself with my advancement, which I might add, was to the benefit of all my working brothers, I rather neglected young Arthur. To be truthful he frightened me. He was so quick, so clever, such a bright lad. His ability to catch hold of something almost before it had been explained to him made me gasp! In consequence, I was wary of his company.

When Livvy's Ma died I was out of work, not that it mattered too much, but I did want to be the breadwinner. So I listened to Livvy when she came up with this idea that I might learn even more about electrics and get out of being a blacksmith, or a general labourer when there was a lack of work. She said it was the coming thing. I had to agree for I had been involved before in the beginnings of it.

It all started at that time when James Barnet's Garden Palace was going to be constructed in the Botanic Gardens. They had to have it finished in time for the 1879 Sydney international Exhibition so they needed lots of men. I went down there, but my reputation as a drinker and fighter was held against me. Livvy spoke to Elaine Pomeroy in John and Pip's firm, for they seemed to have a finger into everything that made money. She hoped that I could get taken on through that connection; Elaine did her best for me, but had to admit defeat.

I moaned to Livvy, who could be hard as flint and never minced her words. She reminded me that my reputation as a drinker was my own fault. She said that if I could gain a reputation as a drinker I could just as easily get one as a specialist worker. She showed me a newspaper where there was paragraph about the use of the new electricity that was going to be used to speed up the work. She said that it would require some real specialist knowledge. She went into the shop and got some books on generating electricity. I remember that they were by a chap called Michael Faraday and a Sir Humphry Davey.

So I read all about the ways in which electricity could be used; and then, when the electric light equipment all came out from England, and was installed by men who came with them, I got a job alongside them. They were pleased to have a labourer who seemed to know what it was that they were doing. It was soon after this that I had to leave Sydney on account of that trouble that I had after a fight.

Now I had put all that behind me, but still needed work. It was Livvy again who came up with the idea of getting back into work with electricity. I told her that there was an opening for a worker with the electricity company. So she arranged for a former electrics worker who had had a bad fall and could no longer do that sort of work, to coach me. Under Leonard Butler's tutoring I made good progress. His experience and the books that we read together quickly made me feel that I could offer myself with some confidence for a post in the developing area of electrical installation.

"Don't forget", said Leonard when I started going after jobs, "Even with your small stock of knowledge you already know more than most. 'In the land of the blind, the one-eyed man is king'."

It helped to have James Barnet's support once again. I had criticised him the first time that I had seen him and he had reminded me that we had much in common. The circumstances were that I had seen him on the site where I was working and asked who he was. They told me that he was James Barnet, and as the Government architect he had planned the building.

"Another member of the class that oppresses the poor bloody workers just because of who they know, I suppose", I said, rather too loudly. I was such an outspoken hothead then.

He had flushed with anger and had come over to me demanding to know who I was. I told him that I was Phillip Gargery, a blacksmith, forced by circumstances to work on more menial tasks than I would wish. He wanted to know if I had completed my apprenticeship. I replied that I had, and that I had worked as a journeyman, so I knew my trade as well as any man there.

He then surprised me, for he said that we were alike, as we both probably had parents who made sure that you were raised to a trade. He went on to say that he presumed that I had worked hard to improve myself, just as he had, and then had come to New South Wales to make something of my life. And that is my history too, he concluded. I said that the difference between us was that he also knew people of influence, and that must be of great assistance to him. For an answer he used his influence to get me more suitable employment.

Now with Leonard's coaching, Livvi's encouragement and a good word from James Barnet I landed a job. It was fairly basic to begin with, but I hoped it would lead to something better in due course. I went around with an older more experienced man to people's houses to do simple installations. The spread of electric light in houses in Sydney was partly due to vanity; it was also a challenge to women's vanity. We were engaged in installing lighting in rich men's houses where they wanted to impress their guests. Nothing much changes, does it?

Something did change though as far as Livvy was concerned. She became involved in what she called women's suffrage. I indulged her. She had been a great help to me in my strivings to better myself, so why should I not let her go to these meetings even if they would never ever come to anything. It kept her happy. I was more contented, if not exactly happy, in perfecting my new skills. That's the secret of how to treat women. Let them think that what they are doing is important, even if it isn't.

Chapter 2

The well off classes, who had achieved their success by the sweat of the workers, lived in grand houses in and about Sydney. Wanting to show off their wealth, they would have a lamp, or lamps, put in by the likes of me along with my guv'nor, who happened to come from England. Some of the more experienced men came from France. Once the lights were capable of being switched on the rich man would get his wife to invite their friends to dinner. As the daylight went candles were brought in, or lit, if they were already on the table. Then, to everyone's amazement a servant, following a prearranged signal, would switch on the new lights.

I overheard a woman talking to her husband in one large house where I had gone back to adjust the switches. While I was engaged in this, he said:

"That surprised them Mattie when I turned on the light as Edward served the dessert, didn't it?"

'Not as much as it surprised Edward who nearly dropped the bloody pudding!' I thought to myself, having spoken to Edward as he let me into the house. I got the whole tale from him and now I was hearing it again. As he spoke to his wife, the master of the house grinned at me. I thought that he was just an overgrown schoolboy with a new toy, but I was learning to keep my mouth shut, so I pretended to be busy.

His wife was less than enthusiastic about the new lighting, despite the fact that she was one of the first to have it installed.

"But Charles, our candles that I chose so carefully made our dining room so pretty when they were lit, and then your electric light was so harsh. I quite feared for the way in which my complexion was shown to it's worst advantage. I was so pleased that I knew to use a little cosmetic aid beforehand."

Charles looked at me as if to say 'women'. I diplomatically kept my head down. I did not want to be drawn into a fight between husband and wife. Besides, I expected a good tip if what we installed worked well when I was finished. Nothing much changes, does it?

"And Anne Marstom was really cross. She declared that such a bright light quite upset her digestion."

"Not enough to refuse a second helping of dessert I noticed! I don't know about her digestion, but she looked rather, how can I put it, drawn?"

"Oh! Charley. You are naughty, but she did look positively haggard in the new light."

He laughed. She laughed. I said nothing except thank you when the expected tip, smaller than I had hoped for, was discreetly slipped in to my hand.

"Tight buggers aren't they? Remarked Edward as he let me out. His sharp eyes had seen just how little had been slipped to me.

I went back to the office to collect the list of my next jobs, thinking as I went how I had changed. There was a time when I would have been insulted to be offered a tip. Now I expected one. It was not as if I had lost my belief in the integrity of the workingman; when times are hard some extra money is always useful. I was getting older too, but I was still ready to strike a blow for freedom when it was demanded of me. I was to find that would be sooner than I expected.

As well as the list of jobs I found two letters waiting for me. The first that I read made me very pleased. It was an invitation to come for an interview at the main depot. I had read in a newspaper that approval had been given for the construction of a new electric tramline from the Semi-Circular Quay and Pyrmont. It seemed that many more men would be needed and I was being considered. Because electrification of all existing steam tramlines was now to be undertaken, there would be a considerable amount of work available. Hurrah to that, I thought.

The second missive made me frown.   A passing workmate seeing my face said:

"What's up mate? You in trouble?"

I told him that everything was fine, but inside I knew that it was anything but fine. Somehow my past intemperate comments and my involvement with the Kelly gang was known to someone, someone who wanted to use that knowledge to my disadvantage. The letter did not say who it was who knew about my past, but gave enough details to convince me that they knew enough to spoil my chances of getting a really good job.

I had run away from Sydney taking at first the name of Abel Magwitch to confuse my pursuers. Later on I changed my name several times and I travelled around as a blacksmith. It was while I was doing a small job that Ned Kelly recruited me. I found that he and his gang were something of folk heroes, as many of the police at that time were absolute bastards and carried out their duties with a lack of humanity that served the gang well. Many people saw them as taking a stand against inhuman authority that they thought they had left behind in Ireland or in England.

As a blacksmith I could make exactly what Ned wanted as long as I had a supply of sheet iron and charcoal. These he promised to get me. He collected old ploughs that he said had been given to the gang by supporters. I used them to help him construct his now notorious armour. Someone knew that I had done this, and in the letter they described just how I had set about the task, proving to me that whoever had written the letter knew how I had been involved

Chapter 3

I went home feeling hope for the future and worry about my past. I puzzled over who it could be that knew about my dealings with the Kellys. Was it the police? Maybe it was one of his brothers? It could have been anyone that Ned or the others had talked to. I stopped thinking about it as I got home. There was no one there, but soon after I arrived and had washed my face and hands Lizbeth, one of our oldest friends came in.

She told me that Livvy had gone out taking Art with her. She was involved in some nonsense to do with the woman who had looked after her Ma just before she died. Lizbeth put together my tea for me then said that she had to go as her husband was expecting her. I thanked her and ate the meal, reading the newspaper the while to try to keep myself calm. I was still worried about that second note so I was a bit short with Livvy when she came in.

I asked where Art was. When she told me that she had left him behind with some blacks, something inside rose up and almost made me choke with anger. I realise now that I was so worried about my own concerns that I let rip at Livvy just because she was there.

"In God's name Liv, I shouted, "what do you think you are playing at?"

She looked scared. I had often been angry but I don't think that I had ever shouted at her so loudly since coming back to Sydney. The real truth was that it was I who was frightened. I calmed down and told her that I had a problem at work and that I had to go back immediately to deal with it. I told her that she was not to worry about, it but should get hold of the carter that we used to collect stock from the docks, and go immediately with him to collect Art. I wanted her to have someone dependable with her, someone I could trust. I know that I should have gone with her, but I thought that I had to sort out my problem immediately. I never thought for one moment that she would return without him.

I told her once again to go and collect Art. I added that I would not be at home when she returned as I had some urgent matter to attend to. I looked again at the note and set out straight away, only pausing to kiss her and tell her that I was sorry that I had lost my temper. The note said that I was to go to the Ultimo Power House and that I was to be there by seven.

It was a beautiful evening, warm and calm. It had rained enough to lay the dust as I had sat and waited for Livvy to come home. Now as I walked along to the powerhouse I breathed in the air and began to feel more optimistic despite the contents of the note. I thought to myself that I had overcome other difficulties in the past. I had been a fighter. I was a fighter still. I would face up to this one and refuse to throw in the towel. Had I known then what I learned later I would not have felt so positive.

I took a tram, but got off it for the one before had come off the rails and everything was being held up. The warm soft air was now getting warmer and dustier. That's how it was in Australia; you might expect it to get cooler at night. Instead it would confound your expectations and the heat would go up.

I pushed through knots of onlookers where there were murmurs from the women about the horses that had been injured. The men looked on silently, no doubt thinking that not so long since it was men who were badly treated. I thought about the letter and remembered how it had come out that O'Farrell, the would-be assassin, had turned out to be insane, and still they hanged him.

When I arrived I was early, so I took out the letter and read it once again. It was the part in the middle that worried most.

> *We know that you helped Ned Kelly and that you used the ploughs of the people who were for him to do so. He would have wanted you to help us, and it has not been forgotten what you said about poor O'Farrell who tried do away with Prince Alfred.*

I was just putting it back when two men, whose cotton scarves were drawn up about their faces came from round the back.

"You are to come with us", said the taller of the two. He looked familiar. I thought that I recognised his voice too.

"Alec", I said. "It is you Alec O'Donnell isn't it?"

He hesitated, then, with a gesture like naughty child that had been caught out, he pulled off the scarf.

"I told you it was a stupid idea to hide our faces. I said that he was sure to know us. Come on Con, take it off."

Con Fleaghly pulled off his scarf too, and the two men, who I knew from having worked with them in the past, glared at me.

"Anyway. You must come."

"And why would I be after doing that?" I asked mockingly.

" Oh Jesus Mary and Joseph! Come now Phillip Gargery, don't be a bloody fool. You know that there are two of us, and that if we two don't take you, we can either get more, or we can get you taken up by the authorities that some have heard you rant against. You may think the police are not interested in the likes of you, but when we have finished telling them all we know..."

"...or all that you will make up", I went on bitterly, having seen something of this sort of activity before where good men's words had been so twisted the police could easily make a case that no magistrate would refuse.

"Ah! come now. Don't be making it difficult for all of us. Christ knows, life is difficult enough without you adding to it."

They were right. I really had no choice. I had to go with them, but I thought that I might persuade whoever was their leader, for these two idiots were plainly simply doing what some one else had instructed to do, that I would be of no use to them. Then I changed my mind. I am not a weakling. Hoping to take them by surprise, I lashed out catching Alec off guard. He fell back and I pressed home my advantage, hitting him. Down he went like a sack of meal.

As I said, I am not a weak man. After all I was a blacksmith and a prize fighter, and I have kept myself fit, but even I had to give up struggling when a third man seized me from behind and held a knife to my throat. If I struggled now I could end up with my throat cut and my body dumped in the harbour.

A cloth was drawn over my head as all three men held me cutting out the light. My hands were drawn behind me and I felt cold metal on my wrists. I shuddered.

"That's right", said the third man whose face I had not even glimpsed, "they're gyves. They were used to hold the convicts; they work well on such as you."

As he spoke further irons were place on my legs. Burdened now with the very metal from which I had made a living in the past I stumbled along in response to their urgings. I was led down some stone steps where I almost fell at the bottom for I stepped down expecting another step and instead came to a stone floor. I smelled dust and decay. I was somewhere that was not normally used, I guessed.

My head was uncovered. It took a while to get accustomed to the meagre light that a tiny oil lamp provided.

"No electric light here", sniggered Con.

Alec said nothing. He seemed to be recovering from the blow that I had felled him. Of the other man there was no sign. They both went back up the stairs leaving me. I heard a door slam.

I looked around. It was a cellar about eight paces by ten. I knew of such cellars having been in a few in the course of my work. This one was not used, nor had it been used for some time. I backed towards a wall and slid down it trying to find a comfortable position to sit. I began to realise just how uncomfortable it must have been for transported convicts in the past. Some even made the whole journey in the ship shackled in this way!

I was quite calm for I told myself that I had been in difficult situations before and knew the value of keeping my head. I had panicked that time when Toby had urged me to run. I was not going to panic this time. I stood up and looked around carefully. What I needed was a long thin piece of metal. A nail would serve admirably. I moved about as far as was able to in my shackled condition carefully running my hands over any area where I might find a nail. The metal gyves on my wrists and the chains on my legs began to chafe, so I drew my clothing through them as much as possible to relieve it.

At the bottom of the stairs I found just what I needed. It was a nail protruding from a wooden wainscot that was poked out sufficiently for me to get a grip on it. Using the gives I worked at it trying to loosen it, and praying all the while that it would not break off. Suddenly the door at the top of the steps opened and a pair of boots came into view. I backed away from my nail as the boots were followed slowly by rough trousers, and, finally a shirt, where a red bandana completed Con's outfit. He was carrying a bowl that steamed.

"Here you are mate."

I shook my gyves at him.

"Yes. Wait while I put this down."

Con set out on the floor a bowl of stew. He then passed a chain through my leg irons and attached it to a ring-bolt set in the wall. Satisfied that I was not able to get away, he undid my gyves and let me bring my hands around to the front. There he replaced them once more.

Now at least I could eat the stew which I did right away for Con provided me with a spoon that was stuck in his back pocket. He saw my look as he wiped it on his shirt first, and laughed.

"Beggars can't be choosers, cocky."

He went up the stairs and brought down an earthenware jug of water. I drank deeply from it as I was thirsty and the stew was salty.

"Sorry it's only Adam's ale, but..."

"...beggars can't be choosers", I finished for him.

At least he provided me with a blanket before replacing my gyves on my wrists behind me. He then took off the restraining chain so that I could hobble around once more before he went up the stairs. Then, before he shut the door, a bucket came tumbling down with an almighty clattering to come to rest at my feet. So I was fed, watered, provided with a blanket and had sanitary arrangements.

What could I deduce from all the foregoing? Well, I was obviously here for at least a night. The noise of the bucket thrown down the stairs had not been a problem for my captors, so it was probably no use shouting for help. And seemingly, they were intent on keeping me alive.

I had slept on just as hard surfaces as this cellar, so I knew that I could sleep when I had completed my self-imposed task with the nail. I needed to sleep if I was get away, and if I did not get away, I still needed a clear head. I returned to my nail. Using my gyves I worked it up and down and from side to side.

It took a long time, and several times I wearied so that I almost gave up the enterprise. Then Con's face and comments came into my mind and I returned to my labours. I would beat that bastard; I would not let him win. It took some days in fact, days when only working on the nail kept me from losing my mind. What I did lose was all sense of time, so that, while I knew that days had passed, I did not clearly know how many.

Eventually it came out and fell onto the floor. Sitting down I managed to get my fingers around it and pick it up. Now I had a tool. I had worked long enough as a blacksmith to know something about gyves manacles and padlocks. Any straight piece of rigid metal could often serve as a picklock. I had seen many a set of twirls in my time and my nail was a poor substitute for them, but I had three things on my side to outweigh the disadvantage of a poor tool: knowledge, skill and strength.

146

When I had run off from Sydney that time when I thought that I had killed someone in a prize fight (it was a trick set up by Toby to get me to run so that he could get at Olivia), and fetched up with the Kellys, I had been on the road as a jobbing blacksmith for some while. You would be surprised how often I was asked for help over a lock or a padlock. Usually they were rusty, and so an immersion in oil allowed me to get them working again. I would not use the key in case it broke off. Sometimes the key was lost anyway. Instead I would pick the lock or padlock, using a piece of steel to probe the guts of the article I was asked to open until I levered back inside as many bars as I needed to get it open.

Using my nail I managed to get the gyves off my wrists. They were so old-fashioned it was laughable how easy it was. I rubbed my wrists. They were not too badly cut about. The skin was broken but the cuts were not so deep that they were a worry to me. I started on the leg irons and in no time I had them off too.

For a while I sat and considered my situation. At least I knew that Livvy was safely back home with Art by now. With that thought I wondered what they would make of the fact that I was not there to greet them. I sat against the wall and must have dozed off. I woke stiff and cold, so I used the bucket, then stretched out on the floor and covered myself with the blanket and fell asleep.

Chapter 4

It was the door opening that woke me. I cursed myself for not having woken up before as I wanted to be really ready when anyone came near me. At least I had the gyves and leg irons hidden under the blanket. There were footsteps on the stairs. Whoever it was came closer and called my name. I pretended to be asleep. He called my name again and prodded me. With a roar I lurched upwards and despite his clumsy attempts to avoid me I managed to knock him down. I fell on him and pressed the leg irons against his throat.

He lay still. He had given up. He had been so surprised at my attack that I had not only knocked him down but I had knocked all the fight out of him. He lay still as I pressed against his throat. I could have easily pushed harder and he would have been a dead man. I needed him alive.

"Now Cocky, get up slowly", I said, and we will go out of here."

I steadily released the pressure on his adam's apple and he rose moaning piteously. I could see that I had bruised him badly. He whispered to me that I would not get away. His throat would not let him speak any louder. I told him that we would see about that. I slipped the gyves onto his wrists.

Pushing him before me I followed him up the stairs. I wanted to use him as a shield. To be honest I was afraid that I might be shot. I was careful not to let him push back or leap ahead. We reached a room that was at the back of a shop. He turned smiling at me and I saw at once why he was smiling. His two companions were waiting, and sure enough, each had a pistol that was trained on me.

"Let him go."

I had no choice. I pushed him forward and he fell in a heap before me.

"You see. I told you he would escape. He's not a man to bugger about."

The older man nodded in agreement.

"Right, Phillip Gargery. You'll do. You'll do very well. We have a job for you.

"And what if I don't want it?"

"Oh! You'll want to do it, won't he boys?
He continued in a mocking tone:

"You see Phillip Gargery, also known as Pip, we know where your son, Arthur, also known as Art, and your wife, Olivia called Livvy by you and those who know her well, happen to be.

He laughed at my expression for I made no attempt to hide my dismay.

"No", he went on, "they're not at home safe as houses, but we know where they are, don't we lads?"

His voice changed and became steely.

"And, if you don't mind us and do what we want you to do, you will not see them again."

"How do I know that you are telling me true?"

He slipped the gun into the waistband of his trousers. He stood aside making an elaborate show of letting me go.

"Go home, and when you see that they are not there and that we are not lying to you, come to the power station again, but this time be ready to do as we say."

Chapter 5

I felt dreadful as I set off back home. Inside I hoped that he was wrong, but the confidence he showed in letting me go free worried me. I came to the shop and as I approached it Elaine Pomeroy came out. She seemed flustered to see me. She gathered her skirts around her as if to make off.

"Is Livvy home?"

"Why do you ask me that?"

"Because you have just come out of the shop, and in the past you always seem to know whatever is going on, even others do not."

She smiled knowingly.

"Yes, that's true enough. And you're right. I do know. She has gone to collect young Art."

"Yes, I know that she went to do that, but she should be home now."

"No, you don't understand.   She came back again without Art and had to go to get John Adam to help her. Now she's gone again but this time she's gone with Wollomba and Jack King."

"Wallomba, that blackfella drunk ? And who the hell is Jack King? And why did she not simply do as I told her and come home with Art?"

I could feel myself get angry. A rage began to grow in me despite my attempts to control it. I didn't understand any of this. Elaine, seeing my anger said nervously:

"Let's go in. I'll explain."

Inside the shop Lizbeth said:

" Oh Pip, I am sorry to hear about Art and livvy having to go to see her brother in Perth. I am keeping the shop going though."

Elaine pulled me through into the parlour before I could reply to Lizbeth. She shut the door and pushed me into a seat and told me to wait until she had made some tea. I tried to ask her what was happening. She shushed me rather as one would shush a child. I began to feel like one.

"I had to tell Lizbeth something. John Adam insisted that it should all be kept secret, but Lizbeth was curious so I made up a story that Olivia's brother, Jamie was not well to keep her quiet. He is in perfect health as far as anyone can tell, him being in Perth and it being so far away."

"Elaine", I said as quietly as I was able, "I don't understand any of this. I'm completely confused. Are Alec O'Donnell and Con Fleaghly anything to do with all this?"

154

It was her turn to be confused.

"Those two? No not at all. Listen and I'll explain. I know the whole story for I made Livvy tell me everything. I could see, poor lamb, that she needed to confide in a woman, so I wheedled it out of her, all for her own good, of course.

"Of course."

"It all started when Olivia began to get interested in aboriginal culture. I knew, of course, that no good would come of it. Well, what she didn't know was that Mrs Dujane, you know the woman who looked after her Ma in that home, was being used by the blacks. So when you sent her back to get Art and bring him home, just as you instructed her, she was told that Art was being held as a hostage. You see, the blacks want their land back. They reckon that it is theirs by rights and that we have stolen it from them. The very idea!

She was afraid to go to the police, as she was scared that they would go gallumping in and start shooting, so instead she said that she would tell someone important who would deal with it. I think that she honestly thought John Adam could do it for her. I must say, I'm partly to blame for in the past I've told Livvy a thing or two about John Adam and how he's the man to get something done when its needed."

I stood up and said:

"Well, John Adam is certainly an influential man, but even he can't give them what isn't theirs."

Elaine made an impatient movement as she folded her shawl over her hands.

"Do you want to hear the rest of it or not?"

I sat down and said meekly:

"Go on."

Livvy went to John, as I said, and he said that he would help but that it would all have done by negotiation. That upset Livvy as she thought that somehow John would act immediately. She was appalled at the idea of talking to the blacks. She imagined that John would have used his position as a big important businessman. She told me that when John got married to that bitch Marietta Rossi, quite a few very important people were there who seemed to hang on his words. You remember that, don't you?

I remembered it well. Elaine had been there too and had told me all about the nasty backgrounds of some of the guests.

"Well, John said that he would get Jack King, one of his most trusted employees to go with her. She insisted that she had to go too. She wanted to be there so as to be able to bring her son home herself. To be honest, I think that she felt guilty as it was her that had got him into this mess in the first case, but I don't think it does to make judgements, so I'll say no more on that subject. Jack didn't want to have Walloomba with them, but John Adam insisted, saying that he would be valuable as he could track like no other could."

"I can't believe that Livvy didn't think about going to the police. Are you sure that she was afraid that they might rush in and spoil things?"

Elaine hesitated.

"Well it pains me to say it, but I don't really know. I thought that I did, know the reason, that is, but now I'm not so sure. As you well know, I pride myself on being well-informed.

I had to smile at Elaine's choice of phrase. Everyone who knew her knew that being 'well-informed' meant poking her nose into everyone's affairs, and she was a terrible gossip too; what was the point of finding out secrets if you couldn't pass them on? Look how she made sure that she waylaid that man who came to tell John Adam about Pip Pirrip's bravery on the Georgette when it sank.

"I can only assume that there is some deep secret that prevented John Adam from pulling strings behind the scenes as he always has in the past. Anyway he agreed that she should not go to the police."

"Who is this Jack King?" You don't need to tell me about the blackfella. I've seen him more often drunk than not outside our shop.

"Jack King is John Adam's most successful proteshay. He had him trained as a geographist or something like that. You know how the firm has such wide interests now, well Jack King is the man that they send out to nose out where there is gold or similar precious deposits; but what could be more precious than gold I do not know."

Elaine paused.

"That's it! That's why John Adam wants it all kept quiet. This demand by the blacks to have their land back must be connected with some deal where John Adam bought their land."

"Or maybe", I said to Elaine, "John simply took it!"

Chapter 6

Somewhat reassured by Elaine's explanation I still found myself undecided about what I should do now. Part of me wanted to go straightaway to John Adam and confront him about his high-handed decisions. I wanted to face him and challenge him to explain why he thought it right to meddle in my family affairs. On the other hand I knew that if I did not return to the power station today my future as a worker able to support my family was seriously threatened. I thought that I had left the past behind me, just as I had left England to make fresh start here in Australia. Now I was discovering that this was impossible; your past always catches up with one in one way or another.

I stood up. Whatever I did, I had to do it now. I decided that even if I did see John Adam, nothing would be achieved by such a meeting. Livvy, Art, Jack King and Walloomba would still be out there somewhere, and I had to trust that Jack King would fulfil the trust that had been placed in him when he had been sent to rescue Art. At least I knew that the threat about Livvy and Art was not real. The letter with my details about how I had helped Ned Kelly was though.

Elaine had to go so I said goodbye and went upstairs to wash and change. I came back down cleaner and tidier, but still not too sure about what I should be doing. I picked up a bottle of rum and set it back down again; I had tried that solution too many times in the past. It was not the way to get results.

It was still only three o'clock as I went into the shop. There I found Lizbeth. I did not want to lie to her, so instead I simply asked if she could manage while Livvy was away. She told me brightly that it was a job that she could manage with ease. She added that Leonard would also help out if necessary. I said that I had to go back to work, a statement that she accepted without question, and she also made no comment when I added that I might be away for a little while. I could see that I was leaving everything in safe hands so I quickly made my way back to the powerhouse.

There I found the three men who had tried to keep me locked up, but now they had a tighter hold over me than the chains that they had previously loaded onto my wrists and ankles. I had easily wriggled free from them; getting free from these men who knew my past would be less easily accomplished.

I decided to go on the attack. I would take the initiative. I spoke roughly:

"So, what is this all about? Why is it necessary to involve me?

"It's about doing something to help your fellow workers. I'm sure that you have heard about the strike by the herders."

"Yes, it was in the papers. They had to give in eventually, didn't they?"

"They had no choice. We on the other had do have a choice."

"To go on strike? Withdraw our labour?"

"To strike, yes, but in a different way."

"What do you mean, in a different way? What other way is there?"

"We can strike at the heart of Sydney. We can blow up a building where electricity is being installed to make them see that we are a force to be reckoned with. It will be a blow for freedom!"

"How so? How will blowing up something that we are building change anything?"

"It will make them think. It will make them take notice of us. It will be a message that they cannot take the working-man for granted any more. We will make this land over into what it should be. For too long now it has become just like England; a country rotten inside, riddled with hypocrisy and run by an elite who are prepared to grind down the workers in order to maintain control. They used to do it with hanging and the lash. Now they simply pay such poor wages and provide such poor conditions that it's almost as bad as it was when we first came here."

I must own that I was stirred by this speech for I had often said similar things myself when younger. When I had fire in the belly it provided no end fiery language. But where did it get me? Where did it get any of us? Look at poor Ned Kelly. I grant you that he believed that he was acting on behalf of others who like him suffered in the hands of a corrupt and vicious police force. But he went about it in the wrong way. Maybe there was no other way then, but now we had other methods of getting our message across.

My problem now was that they believed that I still sympathised with the sort of action that the Kellys took. If I denied this and turned my back on this action I could still be denounced, and I knew that such a denunciation would go ill for me. Men could be found who would swear that I was a troublemaker. The police would be delighted to have in their grasp such a character. Once they had me I would be made an example of.

I knew that I would have to dissemble, to gain time. I would have to pretend to go along with their crackpot scheme until I could safely reveal it to the authorities. Oh yes, I hear you say, you are ready enough to blow on your own kind when it's your skin that you are trying to save. But consider this. They were contemplating blowing up a building, with all sorts of people inside.

"What if some one gets killed?"

"Every revolution has its martyrs."

"I'm not talking about one of us. I mean what if an innocent person gets killed?"

"Phillip Gargery. Don't talk to us about innocence. If they are not with us we have to assume that they are against us. They may be innocent in their eyes, but they are the enemy of the working-man."

"How will it be done then? Where will you get the powder?"

"Not powder but that new high explosive that has been invented. Dynamite. We already have nearly enough for our first strike."

Now I became even more concerned. I had assumed that they might have wanted to use me to get the powder for the explosion. I began to realise that I was to be used in another way, and it shook me to hear that more than one outrage was to be perpetuated. Hearing this made up my mind. I would have to go along with this and then turn informer. I had to. I had to think about how I might get away from my past.

I sat in thought. The older man said:

"We know that you are more than sympathetic to our cause."

"I am for the working man, yes."

"Well then, why are you hesitating? When we attack are you with us?"

I felt trapped. My past was still dictating my present. My future was being shaped by those who had no right to such an action. How could I escape? What could I do to get away from this feeling that it was inevitable that I had to give up control of my own life. I decided to go along with their scheme. Then, when the right time came I would put an end to it and make sure that they were captured. I would have to take terrible risks, both in betraying them and in being involved.

It was a long ride into the bush to the place where Con said that he knew we could get the remainder of the dynamite that was needed. At another time I would have enjoyed the journey. The weather had become quite pleasant and I was now pretty well immune to the insects that swarmed about us attracted by the sweat of the horses as they carried us further away from Sydney and out into an area that I had never been to before.

We picked our way along trails that had been used in the past when they were clearing the land and pushing into places where only the blacks had lived. Without the three of them who seemed to exactly where we were I would never have been able to find my way, and I knew that were I to try to make a break for it and to go to the authorities, it was doubtful that I would ever have found my way out. The place was a nightmare jumble of rocks and trees and undergrowth that defied anyone to remember where they were.

Of course we were travelling alongside roads that these three dared not use. It was important to them that were not seen going to the quarry that was our objective, nor back again. It did not surprise me that the quarry was one owned by John Adam's firm. Somehow I knew that he would be involved in this. I asked whether he knew about our plans. That caused laughter.

When we arrived at the edge of the quarry I was told to unwrap the small tent that we had brought and put our tarpaulin inside. Then, while the others went to see how well the quarry hut was guarded I laid myself down and fell asleep. I was awakened by a jubilant Con who now had a leather bag that he held carefully.

He told me that there had been no trouble. A small padlock had yielded easily to a crowbar. In fact I found out later that they had simply torn out the hasp and that had allowed them to get into the workmen's hut. As to the men who should have been there, rather mysteriously, they were absent.

I was instructed to pack up everything. When I asked why we had brought gear to stay the night, Con told me that they thought that we would have had to wait for a suitable time to take the dynamite. As it happened everything had been surprisingly easy.

With everything packed, the others joined us and we began our return journey. At no time did I get the faintest idea of what or target was to be. I was left to muse about where we would strike. When I asked I was told that I would be told in good time. It was all a part of the whole plan. I was taken along with them so as not to be able go and inform on them. I was also kept in the dark so that, were I lucky enough to give them the slip, I would know only what they intended to do and not where.

Chapter 7

Back in Sydney we went to ground in an old house in Cumberland Street in the area called The Rocks. That night they told me that the plan was to wait until it was dark and then we would blow up the Royal Arcade. I wanted to know why they had chosen the Royal Arcade and was told that, as it had so many shops and offices it was an ideal target. Once it was dark and everyone had gone home we could easily gain entry, and because everyone had left, there would be no loss of life when the explosion took place.

I was told that we would have to make our way together to George Street during the day. That was necessary, for if we went at night we would be too conspicuous. We also had to go together as they did not trust me to go through with the plan. Going together meant that I could be prevented from running. Then, we were to dress in such a way that only our clothing would be remembered, not our faces. After we had set the dynamite in place it was planned that we would shed a layer of clothes and these would be left behind. Anyone seeing us going away, an unlikely event at that late hour, would see not four men together, but separate men dressed differently.

In any case, once the explosion had taken place it was hardly likely that anyone would be interested in us. All attention would be on the ruined building. I pointed out that the small amount of dynamite that we had was unlikely to do that much damage. It was the symbolic nature of the event that would be important, I was told.

The following day, two of the men went with me to the arcade. We walked along through crowded streets. I knew that they had at least one pistol, but it was the knowledge that Con was making his way separately with the dynamite that stopped me from making a run for it. Even if I did get away without being shot, Con would still be at large.

Chapter 8

Having reached the arcade we sat downstairs in hot darkness listening to the everyday sounds of the day with sweat trickling down my body, for I was wearing so much to make sure that I was not identified, that I was hot, sticky and uncomfortable. I was also nervous, a strange feeling, for I was not used to being apprehensive. We heard a sound outside the door. My heartbeat went up. How had it come to this that sound that I would normally ignore made me nervous and upset? I began to get angry. I recognised the signs and tried to restrain myself; I knew that if I lost my temper I made bad judgements.

It was Con who came to join us. He had the leather bag that he handled cautiously. That gave me an idea. Both he and Alec seemed not to know anything about the properties of dynamite. They probably thought that dropping it would set it off. I had more knowledge of it and how it was set off and I knew that unless it was set off correctly it was perfectly safe. It all depended, of course on the condition of the dynamite. If it was old it could be dangerous for it might have become unstable.

Con put down the leather bag and said that all we had to do now was wait until it was dark. We sat in silence that he broke eventually with a question about O'Farrell, the man who shot at the prince. He wanted to know why I had been so strong in my condemnation of his being hanged.

"Sure, wasn't it attempted murder after all is said and done?"

I tried to keep my temper under control as I replied:

"O'Farrell was mad. He had recently been released from a mental asylum. Anyone could see that his trial was as a result of the authorities being embarrassed, and that was also the reason why they hanged him within two months. A civilised society should at least have allowed Aspinall to have appealed against the sentence.

"Who's Aspinall?"

"Butler Cole Aspinall was the barrister who defended him."

"How the hell can you defend an action like attempted murder?"

"Well, it really means representing him. The defence barrister tries to put before the court everything and anything that might be said in his client's favour. By the way this was the same barrister who defended, or represented the leaders of the rebellion at the Eureka stockade fiasco."

"I heard about that. Were you there then?"

"No."

"But you were with Ned Kelly. Tell us about that. Was he a madman too?"

I hesitated. From what I saw of Ned he was certainly not a madman, yet he acted with a lack of caution on occasion that would make most people say that what he did was crazy. I thought about those last hours in the hotel where he was holed up with the hostages. If he had been mad he would have harmed them, I'm sure. He didn't. He didn't harm anyone on a similar previous occasion. I think that he was something of an idealist. He really thought that if he just persuaded people how awful the police were they would listen to him. What he didn't see was the fact that if there had not been firm action at that particular then lawlessness would increase. The awfulness was necessary; there were too many bushwhackers at large. Captain Moonlight was one such. After a time in prison he spent some months lecturing on crime before turning to it again. A perfect example of how dangerous it is to try to put reform before punishment.

And yet, they gave Martin Cash, another notorious bushranger, a conditional pardon, even after he had killed a policeman! I heard the Kellys talk about him and the way that he had gone to New Zealand to do so well that he was able to come back to Tasmania to be a successful farmer.

When I thought back to my time with the Kellys, it was not what I did then with them, but other simpler things that I remembered. That girl who gave me the milk. I could taste it now, warm and creamy. That meat she gave me. I remembered with pleasure the cold lamb that had salt put on it before being wrapped in newly baked bread. I could do with some of that bread and meat now, I thought.

The main method of persuasion that was used to keep me with the three would-be assassins was the Colt revolver that the older man kept stuck into his belt. I had heard about these guns, how quick and accurate they were, so I had no wish to try my luck at escaping. What gave me my chance however was both Con Fleaghly and Alec O'Donnell being sent away in the evening by the older fellow, whose name I never learned by the way. He told them to be off, but to go singly so as not to arouse suspicion. I learned later that they left one after the other, but met up in Pitt Street as they wanted to see the explosion. It was ironic really bearing in mind what happened subsequently.

Now there was only one of them, but he still had the revolver and I still did not want him to try it out on me. We sat there until we heard voices. What they had overlooked was the fact that although the Royal Arcade was shut, there were deliveries made at night. The revolver was drawn and waved at me to indicate that I was to keep quiet. We were tucked away in the sub-basement and I thought that no one would want to come down there.

I was wrong. The door was pushed, but as it had been locked from the inside, once Con and Alec had departed, no one could get in.

"That's bloody funny", we heard someone say. Someone else said something indistinct in answer. There was a laugh, then we heard:

"Let's see if George has a key. He has keys to most of the doors here."

We heard their footsteps fade away. My captor unlocked the door and making sure that his colt was trained on me, he beckoned for me to follow him.

"Bring the bag."

I lifted it. I wondered what he would do now. Was he going to abandon the attempt? At the top of the stairs he looked around carefully and this gave me the chance that I had been hoping for. Raising the bag, I brought it down on the back of his neck. All my frustration at being held so helpless was in that blow. It pitched him forward, and such was the force of my blow that he let go of the revolver which skittered across the stone floor.

If I had thought more carefully I should have simply stayed and tried to get him arrested. Instead I bolted. Through the back stairs I went two at a time, down to where a horse attached to a buggy stood. I threw the bag containing the explosives into the back, seized a whip that had been left there and urged the horse into a trot. It looked back at me, clearly unused to a pace greater than a steady amble.

Nonetheless, it responded to my whip and we made away at quite a speed up and out of the outskirts of the town. I had no clear idea of where I was headed. All I wanted to do was put lots of space between me and that murderous revolver.

As I left I didn't notice Con and Alec, who seeing me leave with the bag, knew that the plan had not worked. The silly fools followed me. They would have been better off to have gone inside to look for the man with the Colt. Instead they ran steadily in pursuit; and that was when I became aware of them. It was clearly them. I had spent enough time with them not to be able to recognise the both of them.

I relaxed as they dropped well behind me. My old nag was not fast, but it had enough speed to lose two men on foot unless they were incredibly fit. I thought at this point that I had lost them, then I saw in the moonlight behind me a cart with a horse that was being whipped along.

It soon became apparent to me that they were not trying to overtake me. If I slowed down, so did they. If I urged my poor horse to a greater effort, they speeded up too. I began to understand their tactics. Rather than overtake me, they would follow me until I could go no further, or rather my horse could go no further, then they would close in on me. My mind up to that moment of realisation had been devoid of any semblance of a plan. Now I tried to think of some way that would allow me to escape.

On we went in the moonlight until I turned off the main road and followed a track simply because it was there. They followed me. Rounding a bend I drove under a stand of gum trees. I just had time to set the fuse for the dynamite and get out of the cart when they turned the corner. They stopped. Because I was in the shadows I was able to wriggle away and crouching almost to the ground to hide my movements I ran down a small pathway.

The explosion when it came was spectacular. I had seen similar explosions when large amounts of rock had to be shifted. This time was different. Instead of rock and earth falling from the sky where they had been lifted by the dynamite, it was pieces of men. I turned away and retched as I recognised the ring on a hand that had been torn off the arm of one of my erstwhile captors.

I swear that it had not been my intention to harm anyone. Setting off the explosion was my attempt to create a diversion so that Con and Alec would not have seen me escaping. I think that they must just have got on the cart as it went off.

An explosion like that attracted the owners of a small house nearby who sent a man to fetch a constable. Strangely, he asked no questions when he came, and seemed not to be at all surprised when I told him my story. He patted me on the back saying that he had been a soldier in the Russian war and had seen so many sights like this that it left him quite unmoved, but he understood a man like myself would find it most disturbing.

Chapter 9

I was able now to return to Sydney where I was held by the police overnight. In the morning the superintendent that came down to see me, as I ate the fresh bread and butter and drank the fresh coffee that I had been given, simply told me that I was free to leave. I went straight home. I wanted first to make sure that Livvy was safe and that Art was with her. After that I wanted to see John Adam to find out what was behind all these happenings, for I was sure in my mind that it was he who was responsible for most, if not all of them.

When I did get back to the shop Livvy was there with Art, and was accompanied by a man who looked familiar. He introduced himself as Jack King. I said that he had the advantage of me, as although I felt that I knew him, I could not remember ever knowing his name. As we sat together over the dinner that Lizbeth had prepared, he said that I might have known his uncle's name better. He told me then about his uncle, John King, and how he had gone on the great expedition.

I knew about the contribution that John Adam's firm had made to fund the expedition. I know that the firm was called Adam and Pirrip at that time, but I always knew that John

Adam was the driving force within it. Pip Pirrip was a weak man, in my opinion, ready to be led along by John into any enterprise. Look how meekly assented to be sent to New Zealand when gold was discovered there abandoning Estella. Anyway, I read about the proposed expedition in the Argus, where it said a rich businessman had given a thousand pounds on condition that more money was contributed by others. The intention of starting a fund was to send an expedition to cross Australia from south to north, from the bottom to the top, from Melbourne to whatever was at the top. Not that there was much there, only swamps I heard.

As I said, it was in the Argus, in a copy that Livvy's Ma had. I had watched her unwrap some books that had been sent by mistake to Melbourne and had had to be parcelled up and returned to Sydney. In the paper it said that Ambrose Kyte had put the money up. John, hearing this, wanted to make a contribution, and when he did so Pip tried to persuade him to go onto the committee that had been set up. John refused, saying that he was a businessman. He was ready to contribute as it brought publicity, but going onto committees was just a waste of time, a nonsense that he was not getting into.

Livvy then told the whole story of how she had set out to rescue Art and had been told to keep everything quiet by John Adam. John had insisted that she should be accompanied by Jack, along with Wallomba. At the end of Livvy's tale I stood up and offered my hand to Jack, thanking him for all his efforts. He blushed and said that it was nothing. I said that any man who had saved my wife and child deserved my deepest gratitude. I noticed that Livvy was looking slightly hot and bothered too. I put this down to the wine that we had drunk in celebration. Had she not been so brown from the sun, I'm sure she would have been quite pink!

Lizbeth listened, mostly open-mouthed, only interrupting from time to time when something even more exciting was described. Jack sat through the narration. He only spoke once when Livvy said how well Art had behaved.

"Your son is a hero. You can be proud of him. I only wish that I had a son who was as plucky as he was."

It was now my turn to say what had been happening to me while Livvy had been searching for Art. Before I began I asked Livvy whether Art should hear my story. He was so excited by all the attention that he'd been getting that I thought he ought to go to bed. Livvy gave that would be best if he were to be allowed to stay up. She looked at him severely and told him that if he was to be allowed to remain, he would have to be quiet and well-behaved. She said that she was firm in her mind that he ought to hear my fullest account. She added that she was sure that whatever I'd been involved in, I had acted bravely and honourably. She emphasised this looking at Art.

My tale took less time to tell. I must own that, despite Livvy's comments, I pruned it and shaped it for there were parts that I felt were not for my son's ears, not yet anyway; when he was older I might tell him all the details.

We all sat in silence when I had finished until Jack stirred himself as if to go. I then asked him to stay, saying I thought that John Adam owed us an explanation. I suggested that we went the following day to see him.

"Beard him in his den", said Art.

"Something like that", I replied.

Jack hesitated.

"He is my employer."

"Whatever he is, he still owes us an explanation."

And so it was agreed that we three would go down in the morning and seek to speak to John. We all said firmly to Art that he could not come. I said that he ought to remain at the shop with Lizbeth, if she would kindly mind it again.

The Magwitch Legacy

Jack's Story

Chapter 1

Everyone knew the story; how a camel had shot and killed its owner. I heard it again as preparations were made for the Victorian Exploring Expedition in Melbourne. Seeing the camels there brought the story to mind. They wanted to use camels for the expedition and my uncle, John King, was put in charge of them. But to return to the murdering camel…its owner was trying to load his gun while on the camel's back. The camel twisted round suddenly pulling the man's hand sideways. The trigger was pulled, the man lost some fingers, and a lot of blood, and eventually died.

I was in the crowd in Melbourne at the harbour when the camels were brought ashore from the Chinsura. One man got too close to one and when the camel belched he fainted clean away. He was dragged out of the way and the camels were led away from the ship.

I thought that they were ugly beasts, ungainly, bad-tempered and not at all easy to manage. The Indian Sepoys had them under control though and led them over Princess bridge into town. I raced ahead to see them arrive at Parliament house. I wasn't the only one that was excited by this novel spectacle and the police had to hold back everybody. An event like this was a wonderful chance for people to see something out of the ordinary, and they grasped at it enthusiastically.

When I first arrived in Australia I considered myself grown up, sufficiently grown up that is to say to pay no heed to my mother. I thought I was old enough to make up my own mind about things, for hadn't my uncle John enlisted in Phoenix Park for a soldier when he was fourteen? And here he was now, grown into as fine a young man as ever you were likely to see; and wasn't he in charge of the camels that had been brought from India? So here I was fifteen and as big a problem to my Ma as the centre of Australia was to the whole of Melbourne, and just as ready as he had been to experience adventures.

I had thought about going to him to ask him to get me onto the expedition. What held me back though was the fact that I was not only a trouble to my Ma, but also in trouble with the police. Being Irish seemed to mean to most folks that I was a natural born larrakin, a prejudice that I certainly did my best to confirm. Well to be honest, now that's joke, for honesty and me in those days were ever far apart; but to be honest, eventually my mother grew so tired of my antics that she turned me off. My fighting and running around were all too much for to bear so she disowned me. When anyone asked her did she not have a son when she came to Australia, she would deny it, and I can't blame her, no, not one whit, for I was the very devil of a fellow, that I was.

It might have been better if I had had a Da. I never knew of one. So with no father to take a strap to me and to belt some sense into me I just ran wild. So I ended up in Melbourne where I fell I with a group of lads whose contempt of the law was even greater than mine.

Despite my shyness at not wanting to go to my uncle to see whether I could get a place on the expedition I still wished to go on it. If the good brothers in Ireland considered that they had larruped the devil out of me, they were wrong. Neither had they beaten out of me a desire for adventure. Surely the expedition would want lads like me to fetch and carry. It was always so in the past. Lads would hang around until someone would send them for water or to hold a horse, or any of a hundred and one things that enabled a lad to earn a copper or two.

I knew that John King who brought over the camels from India was my uncle. My mother often talked about him. She was so proud of the way that he had done so well in the army. I lived in his shade. She told me that he was a hero, having helped to put the mutiny down in India when the natives got out of hand and slaughtered their betters, the white men. She agreed with me in one regard however. The blackfellas were no better in Australia than the natives in India. Bone idle, they lay around doing no work at all and frequently abusing their own women. I heard tell that they would kick their wives in the stomach to induce a miscarriage, so that they would not be burdened with children when they went walkabout.

Of course I knew all about the charade that took place when they selected men to go on the expedition. I had a second cousin who was in the police and he let me through to get a better look when the camels finally arrived. I learned from him later on that more than six hundred men applied to go. Of the six hundred, three hundred were finally interviewed, and do you know what? Not one of them was chosen!

I felt better after that, for I realised that, as my cousin was after telling me, it's always like this; everything is arranged by those in charge. They usually run a charade, but no one with any sense is taken in. So bad cess to them, I thought. I shall still hang around the Royal park for it was there that they began to collect everything they thought that they needed. Much later on in my life when I saw some of the blacks stride off into the outback with a skin bag and a spear and throwing stick fot survival, I understood why the blackfellas thought the white man was so ridiculous.

And I was used, just as I had thought I might be. And I must admit I was caught up in the excitement and glamour of it all as I was. It was novel. It was enthralling, captivating. The high point for me was when they gave instructions on firing the rifles. The noise and smell! I was employed to bring up fresh ammunition, for by then they had got used to seeing around, so I saw and heard everything. That night I went to sleep determined to follow them when they set off.

When John King got back to Melbourne I was shocked to see him so changed. I was in the crowd that watched his arrival. I was still estranged at that time from my Ma; we made a peace of some kind later on, but she continued to say that I was no son of hers. It was about then that I was taken on by Adam and Pirrip . Not that I impressed by that Pip Pirrip, who passed himself off as a gentleman to such a degree that I was suspicious of him. No, it was John Adam who saw that I might be useful to him and to the firm. He told me that I reminded him of what he had been like when he had been a boy in the gold-fields, and had started out selling things to the miners.

Don't ask me what my job was. I just worked for the firm, doing what ever needed to be done, and no questions asked. It meant a deal of travelling. I went everywhere.

I was in Sydney that time when Toby came rushing to John for help. I was sent out immediately and took a cab to a house where I'm afraid I terrified the housemaid. I told her that I had come to collect a Mrs O'Brian, then I pushed her before me without removing my hat. Most uncivil I grant you. That was what I was like in those days.

The maid went into the drawing room and said:

"Please ma'am, there's a cab at the door for a Mrs O'Brian."

I followed her in and I said:

"And I'm here to take Mrs O'Brian home."

There were two others in the room, one, a woman, with a red mark on her face. The other was a man, a proud peacock of a fellow whose surprise when I offered my arm to Mrs O'Brian turned to anger when a cup of tea was upset and Mrs O'Brian stood on the cup. I nearly laughed, but I held my laughter in as Mrs O'Brian gathered up some books and a bag and took my arm. In the cab I told her that Effie, the maid, unknown to people in the house, had sent a boy running to her shop. Toby had dashed to ask for help from John Adam and that was why I had come.

That was how I first met Mrs O'Brian and her daughter Olivia. Everyone I knew thought that Olivia was beautiful. I was certainly bowled over by her. She had no eyes for me on that occasion, being occupied with her Ma, and if she ever noticed me on later occasions she never showed it. Why should she? In her eyes I was a nobody, simply an immigrant from Ireland. She could have had no conception how my life had been changed by John Adam.

When my uncle got married I was invited to the wedding and met him properly at last. I'm not sure if he ever really knew who I was. Later on he was very ill and I only got to sit with him because he said he liked to have me there to have someone to talk to. I think that my mother made sure that I was invited to the wedding as a sop to her conscience. It didn't go as far as admitting our true relationship to the world; I was just another one of the family, quite happy to remain as such too. It was a quiet affair. I liked John's wife. It was she who seeing how he enjoyed talking to me, invited me to come and see them. I was, and still am, a good listener. It has been an extreme asset to me to be able to listen when secrets and details about lands and what has been found on them are told me.

So we sat in the shade ignoring the screams of the birds and enjoying the breeze that came in the evening as we drank tea, often with something stronger in it for John's wife saw no point in depriving him at this stage of his life of some enjoyment. I had always admired him, so listening was easy. I would put in an occasional question to keep his reminiscences flowing.

It was during this time that I heard more about his life in India. He had joined the 70th Regiment there and he was part of a force that put down the mutiny, but this was after he had been employed as an assistant teacher in the regimental school at Cawnpore. When the mutiny was over he became very ill. He did not say so, but I gathered that he had been badly affected by some of the things that he had seen and had been involved with. It must have been a bloody time, what with so many Indian mutineers being slaughtered in the fighting or executed in the most brutal fashion afterwards.

He became so ill, that even after he got better it took sixteen months of convalescence at a place called Murree in the Rawalpindi District for him to recover his health. I thought he might almost have had his mind unhinged by the mutiny, and I think that, as a result, he never totally became a well man. There was always a certain fragility about him. It was while he was a convalescent that he met George James Landells who had been sent to India by the Victorian Government in Australia to buy the camels that were to be used to explore the interior of Australia. It was know that there were deserts there, so camels would be useful.

I think that the army were not that unhappy to lose him for he obtained his discharge without any problems in January 1860, and then immediately went to join Landells in Karachi. He was employed by Landells to supervise the sepoys who were to look after the camels. He had had dealings with the sepoys earlier and got on quite well with them, so he would have been a useful man to have around. The whole lot of them sailed for Melbourne aboard the S.S. Chinsurah on 30 March 1860.

He also rambled on about the expedition, not that I didn't know most of what he told me already, for it had been in all the papers, and I had avidly read everything that I could from the day that the expedition was planned. Thank God the Christian Brothers had walloped me into the reading and writing, although I fancy they might have been better pleased had I read the Bible that they gave me when I left Ireland. No, I don't have that Bible; I threw it away as soon as we set sail. I remember chucking it over the side and thinking that I was done with religion forever. It was another bone of contention between me and my Ma.

He said that he really began to worry when the expedition reached Menindee. There was an almighty row there and George Landells said that he was not prepared to stay. Landells had a huge argument with Burke. John King overheard it, but didn't know really what it was all about. He thought however that George Landells was disgusted with the way that the expedition had been run up to that moment.

It all began to show up in Melbourne when they started out. Of course, the seeds of all their troubles were sown in the preparations and in the fact that the wrong men were in charge. He told me more about that later when I got to know him even better. Anyway, it began with a farce when a camel got loose, God alone knows how, and ran into the crowd of onlookers, of which I was one as it happens.

It brought down a lady off her horse; she was riding side saddle naturally, and when the camel ran into her she fell and broke a leg. You should have heard the yelling and the screaming. They immediately looked for a scapegoat and settled on poor Owen Cowen as a consequence. They decided, without any evidence, that he was the culprit; he had drunk too much beer. Now, I knew Owen. Lots of us lads did, and although I grant you that he could shift it, he had to be much drunker than he was on that day in August to be really at fault. But they needed to blame someone so poor Owen was chosen as the sacrificial victim. So he lost his position immediately.

And that's how it went on. The wagons broke down because they were overloaded with too many useless articles. They even took a Chinese gong! What the hell they wanted it for, the Good Lord alone could tell you. I never heard anyone explain why it was necessary to have such a piece of useless rubbish, unless it was to summon all the Knobs to dinner each evening. The camels behaved like camels do; they are difficult beasts at the best of times, but with the constant rain they became even more difficult, despite the fact that they were not carrying anything. That was another thing that they argued about. They were to be saved for the desert so for the first part of the journey they ambled along carrying nothing.

And then, would you believe it, the whole lot of them came to a halt only about four miles outside Melbourne! What a circus! Despite speeches, cheers and brass bands playing them off, here they were stuck in the mud, hardy any distance, and there they stayed for the night.

To be fair it did rain. And the rain turned the ground to mud. And the wagons were, as I said, overloaded. I heard that there were thirty tons of stores on the wagons when they started. I also heard that there was trouble about paying for the stores. I have since found through my experiences, that in any such enterprise there is always someone who manages to keep hold of some of the money as it passes through his hands. I expect that this enterprise was no different.

I knew about this part of the expedition personally for I walked alongside of them in the rain. It reminded me of Ireland, except it was warmer. So when they arrived at Moonee Ponds I was still with them, ready to run errands, as usual. Boys who hang around circuses and other similar events can usually be expected to get employment just doing simple fetching and carrying.

The Sepoys quickly made themselves at home. This was a situation that they were obviously well used to, having been in the British army. They hunkered down, lit little fires with small amounts of charcoal and cooked their chapattis. I sat as near as I could and asked them whether the rain worried them, coming from such a dry place as India. They laughed at me.

They told me about the monsoons when whole villages were swept away. Still, they did at least give me piece of one of their chapattis with some meat in it and vegetables that were so spiced I thought my mouth was on fire. I called out in agony, thinking that I was poisoned. That made them all laugh at me again, so I crept away to see whether I could find my uncle.

Someone told me that they were all meeting together in a tent where they were certainly much drier than I was. I imagined that they were discussing how to make progress in the soft boggy conditions. I strained my ears, but only heard snatches of the discussion, even though there were raised voices from time to time. Unfortunately too many of them spoke at the same time so it was difficult to catch what they were saying in any detail. I did hear someone say something about the camels and how they had to be kept fresh. I had already heard this as the sepoys had told me that the camels were not to be used to carry any thing; they had to be kept in reserve to be ready to cross the desert in due course. I wondered whether they would actually get that far.

As I sat there in the rain and moist heat I could scarcely imagine a desert without any water at all. Could anyone live there? With no one to send me away I decided to tag along at least until we reached Mia Mia. I knew from what I had heard as the expedition was brought together that I would be safe until then. After that who knew what really lay ahead? I would have dearly like to go with them to find out, but I was turned away and had to go back to Melbourne.

Chapter 2

That was the last experience that I had of the expedition, and what I know now I either read in the newspapers or heard from the lips of its most famous survivor. What mostly interested me was what happened to my uncle. He said that it was while they were waiting for rescue that Burke and Wills died of exhaustion and starvation leaving only him to try to bury them. He told me how he had been in complete despair when the others died and he was left alone. He thought that not only had everyone died miserably, but that he had been forgotten and would have as a result as miserable a death himself amongst the black heathens.

Up to then I must say that I lumped all the blacks together, but when my uncle told me something of their lives I began to see that in fact they were all from different tribes, a bit like Germans were different from Frenchies, and the English were not like the Irish. He also said that, in their way they could be quite clever. Well, when it came to living off the land and finding their way about I couldn't hold a candle to them. Come to think about it, they were certainly clever enough to rescue my uncle and to keep him alive.

The blacks were kind to him, despite having no knowledge of God. He forgave them that for they recognised that he was their superior by caring for him. At night he was put into a native shelter that, though pathetic in its crudity, sheltered him somewhat. After two or three nights in this fashion he came to a decision. It was clear that this was where he would spend the remainder of his days, so he resolved to make the best of it. He recalled the time in India when he had been so ill. How on that occasion he had vowed to himself that should he recover his strength he would grasp each and every occasion to live to the absolute utmost. This was the reason that he had left the army and come to Australia with the camels to join what he thought was to be the greatest adventure of his life.

So when he was offered an opportunity to continue to live, even if it meant amongst the dirty Godless heathens whose food was scarcely edible, and barely sufficient to maintain life, he took it. And he also took everything that came with it, including the woman who shared his bed. Naturally, as soon as he was rescued and was able to return to civilisation and the company of decent God-fearing people, he turned his back on the abomination of that sort of life and thankfully tried to forget it.

When my uncle died in 1872 I was amazed at the fuss that was made in the newspapers. It was so at odds with the simple ceremony that took place, and you might have missed the funeral procession if you were not specially looking out for it. It was not until I read the papers that I came to realise that he was so important as he was the only survivor. Now I think that it was less his importance and more their guilt at setting up such a shambles of an expedition that led to the outpouring of feelings and a call for a pension for his widow. The dismal unpleasant weather was also a reason why so few spectators gathered in the streets.

It was at this time that I became fully occupied with the business of Adam and Pirrip, going all over the country by every means, seeking to carry out my orders. I was well enough paid and I squirreled it away for I had no intention to marry. Indeed, you will consider me foolish, but the only woman who I ever thought that I would wish to marry was Olivia.

To be fair, I could have gone to be a member of another expedition at about this time, for a man called Ernest Giles was looking for two men to explore east to west with him. He was thirty-seven and had been a stockman for most of his working life, and that was how I had met him on my travels.

I sat one night by a campfire with him and listened to how he had never struck it lucky in the gold-fields so had to be a stockman instead. Now he came looking for me, as he had been impressed by me, so he said. I thought it was all a lot of blarney to be honest with you. Well, it seems that a mate of his, called Ferdinand, a German I think he was, wanted someone to go collecting plants and suchlike.   Ernest Giles agreed to go; I think that his mind was still full of the prospect of filling his pockets with gold and precious stones along with plants that he collected.

I considered that he was too much of a dreamer for me to trust him. This mate, a Dr Ferdinand von Mueller, was a botanist and had a government job, so wanted someone else to do the dirty work while he sat back in Melbourne in comfort. He offered to pay Ernest out of his own pocket. That really made me suspicious. Where did that cash come from? I could never quite make it out; did von Mueller really only want the plants, or did he want Ernest to spy out the land for him to find the same sort of things that John Adam wanted me to find?

Anyway, I didn't go. He took two other men and they found a glen full of palm trees. They reckoned that hundreds of years ago there had been thousands of such palms. He found other places too that he named. Just think; if I had gone I might have had a mountain range named after me! Later on I heard that he went on other expeditions and earned a medal. So much for my judgement of him, though the last I heard of him was that he'd gone on the Coolgarie gold rush and was so unlucky once again that he had to work as a common clerk. Someone has to keep the records I suppose.

I had heard, who hadn't? that John Adam and Pip Pirrip had started their successful firm in the gold-fields, so I presumed that when he took me on I was to look for gold. I was wrong.

He said to me:

"What do you think is changing this country?"

That was an easy one.

"People."

"Yes, but with what?"

That silenced me. John waited. He was not an impatient man. He was still good looking, but running to fat somewhat. I hesitated I knew that Adam and Pirrip had been involved in railways, and I remembered the story of how John and his wife, Estella, had been in a train when it had come off the lines and she had been killed. Someone told me that their firm had supplied the railway lines. He saw my hesitation. He frowned. Worried now that he would take my hesitation for lack of knowledge, I hurried to say:

"Railways."

He leaned back with a sigh of satisfaction.

"Exactly. They are opening up this country as they are all over the world, just as God has meant us to."

I was quite taken aback after this when John Adam revealed to me his plan to get me qualified. At the time, once I had accepted his offer, I was so busy learning and reading books that it never really occurred to me why he had chosen me. I vaguely thought that he was being generous, and was remembering his own childhood and how he had turned his back on his own parents in Melbourne. His father was a tailor, you know. Perhaps you didn't know that. Now, however I can see how he made me more effective, and bound me to him. I can also see how he had the foresight to have someone like me going about to find where those twin necessities of railways were to be found: coal and iron ore.

I found them too, just as he wanted me to. I also swindled the true owners of the land out of their rights where I found the minerals that he wanted. That was something else that I learned to do. Not a difficult lesson to learn, I might add for I had seen so much of such behaviour from those who held themselves out to be better than I that it now came as second nature to me.

It was chance, nothing more than that, which led to me coming amongst the Yandruwandha. I had heard about them from my uncle who told me that he would have died had they not supported him when he was lost in the interior. He also told me about Yellow Alice. I was not surprised. I knew from hearing the sepoys talk around their fires that better men than he had sired half caste children in India. Indeed, it was said that some of them went on to have good careers there. So his having a daughter by a black woman in Australia, especially by one who helped to save his life, was understandable. And I could readily understand that once he was safely home with his own people that it was inevitable that he should turn his back on them.

But, now here I was meeting that black woman and seeing Alice for the first time. I felt a twinge of conscience. Not I must say, over my uncle's behaviour but about the fact that a child who was half white should be left among these savages. So I went back and told them in Melbourne that there was a half white child who needed to be rescued and that I needed help to do this.

Yellow Alice was ten when she was brought to Melbourne to be a house servant, and taught to read and write. They worked hard to assist her to cast off her earlier life. They spoke constantly to her about how lucky she was now that she was able to live in a decent clean household, but she was a little baggage and she defied many of the efforts to help her to settle down and rejected their encouragement to forget her upbringing. If they turned their back on her for a moment she would take off the good clothes that had been given her and run wild. Naturally she had to be beaten to stop her from ruining her life.

She defied everyone so much that eventually it was decided to move her away from Melbourne where she had several times tried to return to her tribe. She was taken to Sydney, to the home run by Mrs Emilie Kaye for old white people. There she settled down at last, mainly because she was amongst other black girls.

When she grew up she got married, but needed to work so she went back to work at Mrs Kaye's home. There she looked after Olivia's mother, Mrs O'Brian. And it was there that she overheard Mrs Kaye telling Mrs O'Brian about her early life in England.

Everyone knew that Mrs Kaye was a lady who had come to Australia with her brother. Some also knew that she had worked with lepers. Mostly though, they knew that she had worked in Paramatta which was where Olivia had worked too when they lost the shop to Toby.

Olivia met Mrs Emilie Kaye when she was employed in the Girl's School. As second in charge at the industrial school in Parramatta she had quite a deal of power and influence. She used that to prevail upon Olivia who was worried about her Ma who seemed to be losing her wits. It was an episode when Mrs O'Brian nearly set alight to herself and was doused with water by Lizbeth that finally made Olivia decide to find her somewhere. She was unwilling to have her shut away.

This was at the time when her husband had come home only to have to run off again because of Toby's death. To add to her problems, her only brother had gone to Perth to work, so she felt increasingly isolated. She considered going to John Adam, but gave that idea up because at that time he was having problems of his own. His wife was leading him a merry dance and his son was turning out to be a bit of a wastrel.

It was the natural order of things; servants almost always overheard what went on in any house where they were employed. And usually they kept their mouths shut. There was an unspoken assumption that what they heard they told no one because they owed their loyalty to their employers. Even the bulk of convicts that had been transported and found that they were now servants carried on this tradition. And do not be persuaded that having been transported that they were all criminals. Many were honest enough, or at least would have been honest given the chance. It was surprising how many still felt that they owed their allegiance to the royal family.

Mrs Dujane, born Alice King, who was also called Yellow Alice, felt that she owed no allegiance to anyone at all. Abandoned by her father and brought into what she considered to be slavery, she held within her such a seed of bitterness that belied her looks, for she was an attractive woman. That seed was to grow. In the meantime the subtle mixture of blood had produced a face that made many a man turn and look. Her nickname, Yellow Alice, was a reference to her paler than usual face. And all the while the seed of bitterness grew within her to be eventually a flourishing plant of resentment.

So when she overheard the conversation between Mrs O'Brian and Mrs Kaye she wrote it down and held on to it thinking that she might be able to use it later in some way. Bearing in mind what everyone thought about Mrs Kaye, it was particularly shocking.

When Mrs Kaye had finished telling her story she waited for Mrs O'Brian to make some comment. She was either too shocked or too diplomatic to do so and stayed silent.

Eventually Mrs Dujane heard Mrs Kaye say in a low voice:

"What do you think I should do?"

Mrs O'Brian replied that she did not know what Mrs Kaye should do, then said that, were she to write it all down and give it to someone to read, she might find that would help to soothe her somewhat.

I suppose that I tried to help Alice King because of my family connections, but I also tried to help others. One such was Edward Jones. Now if Walloomba was a drunk, so was Edward. The truth of the matter was that we all felt sorry for him and could see that he really needed friends. No matter what we did though he usually ruined it by drinking. I suppose he got a taste for it when he was sent to Brazil, if he ever was in Brazil.

We all enjoyed his stories. How he had been sent to Brazil as a transported convict. What a liar he was, and yet, how we enjoyed his lies! I mean to say, everyone knew that if you were transported it was to New South Wales in Australia.

He claimed that he had to be transported because he had broken into Buckingham Palace where he had hidden himself under a table and watched the young queen! What is more, he also claimed that he had actually stolen things from the palace, papers that had been bought from him by foreigners. He also claimed that he stole the queen's undergarments! Can you believe it? When he was caught he said that they sent him to Brazil, and the tales he told us about that country were even more astonishing.

Not content with being let off by being sent to Brazil, he cheekily went back to England and walked from Liverpool to London. When we asked him what he lived on during his walk he replied: 'turnips'. When he got to London they sentenced him straight away to be transported here in Australia. You had to like him. I took to him immediately but John Adam was not so keen when I proposed using him and I suppose he was right.

The trouble was he just could not leave the drink alone. I thought he was a tough character, who would be useful, and so he was, but one glass of grog and he was just longing for the next one and so it went on.

Chapter 3

I didn't know what John Adam wanted me to do this time, but as usual, I went to see him when he sent for me. I owed so much to him that I never ever considered saying no. He began by reminding me about the Otlands business. I didn't really need reminding. We had sailed rather near the wind on that occasion but with enough money changing hands, and no-one believing the blacks, we had finished up owning the land where eventually the usual mines were opened up to produce the coal that was needed for the railways.

Now apparently some blacks had got it into their heads that we had stolen the land, despite the fact that it was all done legally. That is to say there were papers to prove that John Adam had title to the land, never mind who said otherwise. Unfortunately in order to force the issue they had taken hold of a white boy who they were using as a hostage to force John's hand. In answer to my question about using the police, John replied that it was a little delicate, and that he would prefer to keep the authorities out of it. I looked at him.

He gazed back steadily. Nothing much troubled him in matters of this kind. He believed that white people were the natural owners of all that existed in Australia.

I was taken aback though when I heard that it was Olivia and Phillip Gargery's boy that had been taken. I knew Olivia from way back when I had rescued her Ma that time. At that time I was really taken with her. She was a beauty, haughty despite being a convict's daughter, as she would constantly remind everyone. It upset her Ma to hear her say so. I ignored it; I was ready to adore her, but I knew though when Phillip Gargery came on the scene that I didn't stand a chance. I could see that he was a persistent chap who would never take no for an answer. He seemed to be well in with both John Adam and Pip Pirrip too. Somebody told me, I don't know who, that he was related to Pip in some way.

Anyway, I was instructed to use Walloomba as my tracker and to go with Olivia the following day to bring back Art, who was Olivia and Phillip's son. I have had stranger instructions in the past and managed to carry them out. It didn't worry me that Walloomba was a drunk. I knew that once we were clear of Sydney and he was away from the grog that he would quickly sober up and would prove to be as useful as he had ever been in the past. I just hoped that he had forgotten about the shooting that had occurred the last time we had worked together. Not that I minded him saying anything. After all, it was my word against his. And who was going to listen to a grog soaked broken down black man?

I was more concerned about Phillip Gargery. I knew him to be a blacksmith by training and a prize fighter by inclination. He had knocked out the Tasmanian Devil I remember. It was the talk of the town. John assured me however that Pip, as he was known, would be fully occupied here in Sydney. I need have no fear that he would came charging after us and spoiling any arrangements that I managed to make to settle the matter.

My job, I was told, was not only to get Art Gargery back safely, but also to put a stop to any ideas that these blacks might have about owning land.

It was the final bit of news that John gave me however that worried me most. The land that was in question was Grangeway. On that occasion we had had to press much harder to achieve our objectives. The blacks had resisted us, and one of them died as a result. I managed to get away with it by swearing that he had attacked me and I had had to shoot him to defend myself. Well, I have never held myself out to be a saint; who could be in the sort of business that we were in? But I felt this time that it had gone too far. I tried to make amends by giving some of the money that I made to the tribe, but they gave it back. They insisted that we had tricked them out of their land.

Well, strictly speaking there was some trickery involved, but they had never properly used the land themselves, letting it stay in the same condition year after year. I did notice that they had picked up some of the coal that was on the surface where we later on put in a mine, and used it for fires for cooking. As a matter of fact it was that very thing that drew my attention to the existence of the coal deposits in this area.

Grangeway resembled Morwell where the Gunais lived. They came to notice when the white men came south from the Monaro region of New South Wales looking for grazing land for their flocks of sheep. In time the whites took over the land. There was a deal of squatting went on in the 1840s and afterwards, but it was not until the 1870s that they began to sell off the land properly. John Adam made a mint of money from such sales, I can tell you.

But it was the railway line that ran from Melbourne to Sale that really brought the township of Morwell into prominence. It was the same in many places. All sorts of work became available. Without work there are no wages. No wages no trade. The railway brought work but needed coal; and there was coal in plenty in Grangeway just like Morwell where the Great Morwell Coal Mining Company and the Maryvale Proprietary Coal Mining Company were set up to mine steam coal.

Maybe the natives lost their land, but that's progress; they were welcome to work for there was plenty to do, but they usually refused to do so, preferring to wander around the country as they always had, killing a few animals, burning off the undergrowth occasionally and growing a few crops.

Chapter 4

Because I held myself in readiness in case I was called upon to make a quick foray into the outback, I was able to call on Olivia Gargery the following day pretty well ready to go. I thought that she would probably want to take a mountain of things and I was ready to say no to most of them. She surprised me. She had packed an absolute minimum. She told me that, as she had already spent some time in the bush, she was aware of what was essential and what was not. Though it did not stop her slipping a book into her bag I noticed.

Walloomba simply had a leather bag with him. I very much doubt whether he owned that much anyway. I could tell that he was still pretty well under the influence of drink. I can never remember a time when he wasn't, once we came back to Sydney. Out there, in the primitive countryside he reverted to the simple savage that he was before we whites got at him.

So we set off. I didn't bother to ask about Olivia's husband as I had been told that John Adam would be coping with that side of things. She had a word with a woman of about her own age called Elizabeth. From what she said I gathered that she was being left in charge of the shop. An old man, Leonard, whose full name I didn't catch, was their lodger. He seemed rather put out that Olivia was going off. That was Olivia. Each and every man at her feet, me included, but I was taking good care not to show it.

We made pretty good progress for it was not difficult at this stage to see in which direction the tribe that had taken Art had gone. We moved along steadily and I gave Walloomba his head. It was when we were all resting in a clearing that I got angry with Walloomba. He came back from chatting to these blackfellas that we had met, saying that we were to strike off to the north-east. Even I knew that this would be a bad move. They would not have gone in that direction.

Walloomba insisted. I said no. I said I knew about such places and I told Olivia that I knew about them because I had been at the edge of the disaster that was called the great expedition. She had read about this in the newspapers so had some idea of what I was talking about. I told her that it had been a complete disaster, a fiasco. They covered up what went wrong in order to hide the guilt of the men involved; men who should never have allowed it to happen the way that it did. I suppose I was a bit excited, but I wanted to impress on her what could go wrong. I could see that she was impressed so I suggested that we camped for the night and I told her that I would explain. I suppose too that I also wanted to impress her.

She called Walloomba over and asked if it was a good idea to stop for the night. He said:

"Yes, you must listen to what this man has to tell you, tomorrow we shall go on."

Wallomba said this while putting a hand on Olivia's shoulder. I was incensed. I told her to watch out for him. I added that if he tries to take another liberty like that, I would deal with him pretty smartly.

She told me to stop looking for trouble. She obviously had no idea what these black savages were capable of.

Later that evening, after a meal, Olivia asked me to tell her about the expedition so I set it all out for her. How John King had been my uncle, the famous John King, the only survivor of the expedition. How I had wanted to be involved, but so many wanted to go I never stood a chance. I told her that I had at least assisted in the preparations; these were the ones that her Ma had read about in the newspaper. I was also there seeing them all set off, and even going with them some of the way. I made Olivia laugh a bit when I described some of the chaos of those first few days. I told her that I had seen my uncle on his return. Then, later on when he was very ill, and just before he died, I heard the whole sad true story from him. I told her how I would visit him and sit with him, and gradually he would draw upon his memories and tell me what exactly had happened.

I think that I had made a good impression on Olivia. I wanted her to trust me. I said that if we were to be successful we all had to trust each other. I would have liked her to do more than trust me. Was it so wrong that she might also like me? I think she was beginning to.

Walloomba joined us. I stared at him trying to show that he was not welcome. He sat down and said to me:

"I know you."

"Of course you do", I replied.

"No. I mean I know of you and what you have done."

I stayed silent. I wondered just what he was about to say. I must have shown this for Olivia looked at me in surprise. I had to tell that I did indeed know Walloomba from well after the expedition. I tried to divert her from listening to Walloomba.

"It was doomed you know. Many thought that. Mind you, most never said anything at all until much later after the whole fiasco, then there were mutterings about pride going before a fall."

Olivia smiled and told me that that was one of her mother's sayings.

"Yes, I know that. She said 'Least said soonest mended' when I brought her home that time."

"You brought her home?" When was this?

"I rescued her. Brought her back to your place in a cab."

Olivia stared at me. Walloomba got up and walked away and I felt a great relief at his going. Olivia began to say something then stopped. She frowned in concentration. I could see that she was struggling to remember. Then her face lost the frown that indicated how hard she had worked to bring back into her mind that particular day, and she smiled.

"Yes. I remember you now. You were even slimmer then, dapper, quite the beau."

My face flamed. She turned away indifferent to my reaction. I tried to put it down to the fact that she was suffering badly from the heat and being eaten alive by the insects. I had developed a certain of immunity to these bites having been bitten so frequently in the past. I used to joke that they had found nicer skins than mine to bite. I could see that she had scratched the bites and her skin was swollen. In reality, she really was indifferent to my feelings. Why should it not be so? She was married and had a lad, so why should she even look at me. All the same I felt a pang at her indifference.

Walloomba came back from talking to a parcel of blacks who had been jabbering to him. He told us this time that Art had been seen. He had been here, but had gone up river. 'Thank God', I thought. Now we can veer away from going on an abortive trip into the desert regions.

Olivia seemed upset. I suppose she had thought that she would be reunited with her son immediately.

"Cheer up, it's good news. Now at least we know the direction he has gone. If they have gone up the river, so can we. All we need is a boat. Leave it to us."

I looked at Walloomba seeking his approval. He nodded glumly. I think he was upset that his theory that Art had been taken in the other direction had been proved wrong. I didn't add when I had spoken to Olivia that at least we knew he was still alive, but am sure that it was on her mind.

We went to see whether we could buy a boat. I was aware that the blacks had them. They had a saying, which I was certainly never going to repeat to Olivia, that it was best to seat the oldest women in the back of the craft, as that was there where the crocodiles struck! She went to talk with the black women. I say talk, but it would have to be by signs mainly that she would have to communicate unless she found someone who spoke some English. I knew that she would want to ask them about Art. I expected that it might take her a while.

This gave me the opportunity that I wanted. Before we went any further I needed to get things clear with Walloomba. I asked him to sit down and he did so. I sat down beside him.

"Walloomba, I know that you saw me shoot that time, and I know you think that it was my fault that the man died. What you do not know is that I have been back and paid money to the tribe."

"Blood money."

"Precisely. I paid them the exact amount that they demanded. They are satisfied."

"How do I know that this is true?"

"If you do not believe me, there is nothing that I can say to persuade you otherwise. But what is more important here, to maintain your hostile attitude to me, or to assist me in our efforts to help Mrs Gargery?"

Walloomba suddenly smiled. He held out his hand. I took it.

"Let us see whether we can get a boat", he said.

It took some while. They were not keen to hand over to us their boat as it only just been completed. We bargained for some while. In the end we gave away much too much for I was anxious to get back to Olivia. I needn't have worried. The women had taken pity on her and had produced various concoctions to put on her swollen bites. They even gave her a little pot of stuff to go with us. She put it into the boat carefully along with the other things that she had brought along. One of the things was a parcel. She showed me the contents that night. It was a set of clothes for Art.

Chapter 5

With everything packed in, we got in carefully and began to paddle up river. Olivia sat in the stern. She was a clever young woman for she constructed a little shelter from the sun so that she avoided the worst excesses of sunburn. Not that it mattered. She had already caught the sun to such an extent that she looked more like the women I had seen on my travels who struggled to make a living out of the land that they had been granted. Some of them were quite young, but the land was wearing them out much quicker than Olivia.

We made very good progress. The river was broad and flowed quietly between huge stands of trees. It turned hotter and more humid. Soon clouds obliterated the sun. With no sun you would have thought that it would be cooler, but that's not the way of things in this blasted country. It stayed hot, and just as I thought that we must to stop as it was so wearing, it began to rain. At first it was a few fat drops that plopped into the water, then these increased until you could not see the river's banks. Near to the boat the rain beat until the water looked as if someone had lit a fire under it and it was boiling. I was amused to see that Olivia was trying to use her sun shelter to dodge the rain; it was too much for her, so she gave up and bailed it out instead.

We were about to stop when there was a sudden bright shaft of sunlight ahead of us that hit the brown water, and the rain stopped; just like that. We went onto the bank and made a camp of sorts. I busied myself with making sure that the boat was well secured. Walloomba lit a fire and we had some oatmeal and tea. Olivia seemed in better spirits. She changed the dressings on her bites. She told me that in the past, following that business when that madman shot at the prince at the picnic, she had wanted to be a nurse. It was the Nightingale nurses and the new hospital that was built that sparked off her interest. They turned her down. Her constant refrain that she was only a convict's daughter had told against her. She had refused to be what she had not been, so they took their revenge. She learned a bitter lesson. It's sometimes better to go along with what society wants, even if you think it makes you a fraud. All my life I have felt that; a fraud that is. Even when I became qualified I felt that someday someone would find me out and say that I was nothing but a jumped up Irish tinker.

I said nothing of this to Olivia. I thought that as John Adam had entrusted her to my care that I had better go on pretending that I was as clever as he had made me out to be. We settled down around a fire and at least it did not rain that night. But the following day it did. How it rained! Not the quick heavy shower that we had experienced the day before, but a steady continuous relentless rain. I have seen similar rains in the past so I was prepared for what I knew would be coming.

And sure enough it arrived. The river began to rise. It began to lose the smooth easy lazy passage towards us and became more turbulent. Eventually it overran the banks and spread out either side of us and it became difficult to establish just exactly where the banks were. We saw snakes in the trees that had climbed them to avoid the water. Most of the birds seemed to have flown away. Some animals drifted past, drowned in the flood waters. something else was drifting past and Olivia called out for me to get it. I leaned over and dragged out a white shirt. Olivia was jubilant.

"Look, it's Art's shirt. See his name stitched in at the hem?

If she was jubilant, I was more than satisfied. We were on the right track, but it worried me that the shirt had apparently been abandoned. Why was that? I said nothing to Olivia. Instead I concentrated upon getting along as fast as we could.

Now ahead we could see that tumbling down over a mass of rocks the river fell into a pool from where it poured towards us. As we approached the noise was terrific and the spray was everywhere with small birds flitting through it. On the branches of the trees there were other larger birds. It could have been a model for Eden. Olivia said as much and began quoting poetry. It sounded pretty, but meant little to me.

We pulled over and made sure that our boat was made fast as we were certainly not going to be able to go any further in it. There was no possible way that we could have manhandled it up over those rocks. Instead we skirted round them climbing to find somewhere were we could again stay overnight. It was then that we found the cave. It was not so much a cave as an indentation in the rock. It was not the cave that made us stare at it in wonder however, but the carving at the back that was all coloured in, of a huge serpent!

"This is the mighty serpent who looks after the whole world, and who has arranged it so that that everything has its work to do. You saw how the birds were dealing with the dead animals. Soon the ants will finish what the birds have begun."

Walloomba laughed at Olivia's grimace.

"Not everything in Eden is pretty, but everything has a reason to be there."

I wondered at the freshness of the colour. I was staring at the way that the stone, which I judged to be limestone, was split and partially covered by tremendous tree roots. I looked up at the immense trees that clung to the rocks. In time I could see that the roots would expand and destroy the carving.

Walloomba watching me hold out my hand, said:

"No. Do not touch. It is sacred. At the beginning of the year only those who are..."

He used a word that I had never heard before which he later told me meant 'blessed'. He went on to say that only the blessed could touch the serpent and were permitted to freshen its colours for another year.

I asked what would happen when the roots destroyed the carving. He said that when that happened the great serpent would come again somewhere else. No one could say where that would be, but it would happen. He pointed at the way that the serpents seemed to be swallowing its own tail.

"You see. It never ends."

Olivia said quietly:

"As it was in the beginning, so it will be at the end. World without end, forever and ever, Amen."

She then asked who put it there.

"It was put there much longer ago than any of us can remember. It was put there when time itself began", said Walloomba proudly.

"The great serpent gave it to us to look after, and he made us put him here on the rock to remind us to care for it and to care for the world."

Despite what was obviously a sacred place, Walloomba started making camp there for the night. He had seemed to grow in stature since I had asked for his help, and now had become almost like an elder statesman with the authority that went with that role. Gone completely was the drunken stumbling figure shambling helplessly in our world. In his world he was master.

Now he took charge of us, ignoring any attempt on my part to take control. He used his fire making kit to start a cheerful blaze. I have always been interested in watching how this is done.

Walloomba took his small bow, which was a springy piece of branch notched at each end. Attached to the notches was a piece of finely plaited skin. He then looped the plaited skin round a small hard stick that had a point at one end that went into flat carved piece of bark with a hole at its side. The bark was laid on the ground. The other end of the stick was placed in a stone with a hole hollowed out of its centre. This stone was held in his left hand and it enabled him to bear down onto the stick that he twirled with the plaited skin using his right hand. Backwards and forwards it went at such a speed that the point of the stick got hot from friction. Eventually it got so hot that it began to glow. He had already put some dry moss by the hole in the bark so all he had to do when: lo and behold the moss burst into flames.

"Prometheus couldn't have done any better!" said Olivia.

Not ever having met this Prometheus chap, I grunted and got out some food for us to eat. With a decent fire to sit by, some grub inside her and the thought that we were catching up with Art, Olivia seemed much more cheerful. Her infected bites were less swollen too. Neither of us took any notice of the occasional rustling sounds that formed the usual background as nocturnal creatures went about their business in the bush.

We both ignored a slightly larger sound behind me. Across from me, Olivia's face and gasp of astonishment, along with her looking above my head, made me sure that what she had seen was a person. I swung around cocking my gun as I did so.

Walloomba called out:

"No! and leaped forward pushing my gun down for otherwise I might have shot Mrs Dujane!

Chapter 6

She calmly walked forward, ignoring my gun, into the light of the fire where she simply stood waiting.

"So my message did get to you", said Walloomba smiling.

She inclined her head in answer; then looking at Olivia, she told her that her son was quite safe. She went on to say that he was fit and well, and that Olivia should be proud of him. I could see that Olivia was struggling not to lose control. She was obviously delighted to have such good news, but was, at the same time angry with the bearer of the news for having taken away her son.

Olivia said coldly:

Where is he?"

"Don't worry so. He is safely with my people. I am sorry that I have used you both, but I had my reasons. You see I can tell you now who I really am

Olivia said:

"Aren't you Mrs Dujane?"

"Yes, but I'm also Yellow Alice, and I once was Miss King."

Olivia looked totally bewildered. Mrs Dujane turned to me.

"That's true isn't it?"

What could I say?

"Oh yes! He knows my full story because he is part of it. That man, the one that everyone thought so wonderful; that man, the man who was the only survivor of that great Victorian expedition from Melbourne to discover what was already known by the people who lived there, was my father!"

"You cannot mean John King?"

"Yes, I do mean John King. And this man is his nephew. So you see we are related."

Olivia looked as if she found this very difficult to believe. She looked at me as Mrs Dujane said:

"I'm not a liar, you know."

Olivia replied:

I'm sure you are not.   It's just that...I'm just so astonished at what you are saying. Perhaps you had better tell me everything, then I might begin to understand why you ran off with Art."

"Listen then. When John King, my true father, was nearly dying, In fact all the others were already dead, he was cared for by the Yandruwandha tribe. This was just one of the tribes that tried to help that expedition. No one seems to realise that the whole time that the expedition was making a mockery of itself, the local tribes were watching the foolish white men and sending messages about them to each other."

Olivia said doubtfully:

"How could they do that?"

"We would send smoke signals. They are not the only methods that we can use of course. What do you suppose that Walloomba did to reach me and bring me here?

I looked at Walloomba who stared back innocently at me. I knew that he had done this. God alone knows how. I had seen similar things before when natives had simply walked off into the bush saying that they had to go home. Later on we would find that someone had died or was in trouble and they gone home to be with them. There is a whole lot that we do not understand yet about these primitive people, that's for sure.

Mrs Dujane, sat down now completely sure that she had Olivia's full attention. She asked for some tea. Walloomba gave her some that was rather stewed. She made a face at its bitterness, but drank it down.

"Please go on", said Olivia.

"Every member of that expedition was offered assistance; they were even invited to join in the corroborees; they were offered gunyahs to shelter them. Everything was refused; they would accept nothing, even our food was rejected, except at the very end when they had to accept it or starve.

In the end only John King, my father, was left, and was left so helpless after the deaths of his companions, that he had to be taken to a gunyah that had been specially built for him where he could be cared for. In time he did recover. He started to take a part in our everyday life. He even helped get food for us for he still had his gun. And he took the Yandruwandha woman that was offered him.

She was my mother and John King was my father, and I was known as Yellow Alice. I think my father would have called me Alice, but the Yellow was added to my name by others, for I was not as dark as the other Yandruwandha girls that I grew up with.

I was born in 1862 and lived my first few years in the tribe. To put it plainly my father deserted me and my mother. He walked away from his responsibilities. Like so many other white men who had half black children he simply walked out of our lives. Far better had we been left alone at that time. At least we were accepted. I was brought up in the tribe just like all the other girls. You might not believe it but I was completely accepted by them all. Now what am I? Who am I?

Now, when Jack here was prospecting for things in the land that would make the land valuable he came across me. He was told how a certain white man had fathered me and deserted me and my mother. He says that, as we were related he felt that it was his duty to rescue me and get me brought up correctly. The real truth is that he felt the guilt of his uncle and rescuing me helped him deal with that guilt.

When I was ten I was brought to Melbourne by him to be a house servant, and you might say that I was well treated for I was taught to read and write. But at the same time I was encouraged to forget my upbringing. I was told to forget my tribe. I was stolen from them and from my mother."

Olivia stirred and looked as if she wanted to ask a question. Mrs Dujane raised a hand to stop her. I thought to myself: What is she complaining about? I rescued her. I gave her a chance to better herself, to be able to read and write and speak good English. She was even instructed how to clean so could always be suitably employed, suitably that is for a black half-caste bastard.

"Three years after I arrived in Melbourne, as I was such a nuisance for I kept running off and wouldn't wear boots, I was taken to Sydney where I was given a job looking after old white people. Now I could not run away; it was much too far, so I accepted my fate and worked for Mrs Kaye who was like a second mother to me. Most whites are sinners; she is a saint.

"She helped me get married to a man in the Bediagal tribe and I had a son, as you know well. Now my husband is dead so when I met you Olivia, I was back at the Home because I had nowhere else to go. I thought that you might be like Mrs Kaye and might help me. When you showed an interest in how we lived, I thought that I could use you. I was being pressed to help get some lands back, lands that belong to us."

I couldn't help but break in at this point and say to her:

"You blacks never had any claim to any of this land. Before we came to this country and improved it you just moved about. No one owned it. Then, we arrived and we took it over in the name of our Queen Victoria. If anyone owns anything, she does."

That took the wind out of her sails. She stayed quiet for a moment, said coldly that I might be clever but I was not clever enough. She moved to the back of the cave where the firelight shone on the carving of the great serpent. As the flames flickered, so did the serpent; it seemed alive. Her

226

meaning was clear. Whoever carved this serpent had a claim of some sort. I had to answer her.

"But even if I and Mrs Gargery here accept that there is some merit in your claim, that will be as nothing against those who have papers that show in law that they own it. Lawyers always win, I know. Let me explain how I am involved and why I am so sure that you cannot win.

When I was taken on by Adam and Pirrip, John Adam saw me instead of Mr Pirrip. He told me that recent discoveries in Australia of minerals and other items were the principal interest of the firm. What they wanted to find above all was iron ore and coal. England was being transformed by railways; and he wanted Australia to transformed in a like manner. I was to be used by him for this purpose.

Apparently, following his investment in the great expedition, he had thought that I could find out from my uncle what the expedition had discovered in the way of geological finds. I had to tell him that I was unlikely to be able to talk to my uncle as I was estranged from the family. This stopped him pretty smartish. I was sent away and told to come back the following day."

Mrs Dujane moved, and clearly wanted to interrupt. Olivia jumped in however, saying she wanted to hear the end of the story so I was able to tell them how I was trained as a geologist. I also told them just how I was then used by John Adam. If I found deposits of iron ore or coal I was to report to him and no one else, and he would arrange to buy or get hold of the land where I had found it.

I learned some words in various tribal languages for this meant that the blacks were willing to talk to me and they would show me areas where they knew I was interested in the rocks. I would spend hours or even days with them talking about their land. Of course I knew that when I found something we would take the land from them, but I thought at that time that they are such God-awful lazy fellows that I had no feelings of guilt on that score.

Despite demanding that I finish my story, Olivia was not really paying me her full attention. As soon as I finished she turned to Mrs Dujane and wanted to know more about Art. Mrs Dujane smiled at me as if to say 'so much for you and your clever words'.

"I will take you to him as soon as it is light", she said to Olivia."

Chapter 7

I was not happy at following Mrs Dujane, but what could I do? It was probably our best chance of catching up with Art. I thought that even if we were to get to Art we would still have to negotiate with whoever had him. I said as much to Olivia who replied rather tartly that we would just have to cross that bridge when we came to it. I said nothing in reply and was amazed when Olivia put a hand on my arm and said with tears in her eyes:

"I'm so sorry. I'm getting like my Ma."

Well she could be as sorry as she liked but I was still not fully convinced that this was what we ought to be doing. To add to my apprehensions, Walloomba kept looking back as if he was expecting trouble. When we rested and the ladies withdrew for a moment I asked him outright what was troubling him. He looked shifty and said evasively that there was nothing to worry about.

I walked into the bush so as not to embarrass the ladies. Afterwards, when I was buttoning myself up and still out of sight I heard Olivia ask Walloomba the self same question that I had just asked. He didn't answer but I could see as I peered through the foliage that he was shaking his head.

At least Mrs Dujane seemed to know exactly where we were going. We moved along steadily until we needed another rest. It was as hot as ever I remember it being, and in amongst the vegetation it was also humid. I expected Olivia to demand that we slow down for she was suffering from the humidity much more than any of us. Walloomba simply loped along almost as if he was a machine. I must say, for a black, he was a most useful fellow to have with us. I was beginning to think that he was someone that we really could rely upon. I was soon to put that to the test.

As we sat there getting our breath back Mrs Dujane pointed to some rocks ahead of us saying that the going would be more difficult now as it meant climbing. Ye gods! More difficult? Olivia scrambled along without complaint. I had to admire her. Once or twice I had to hold out my hand to her so that I could pull her up a difficult section. She placed her hand in mine with complete trust. At the last difficult slope that was so steep that it was more of a climb. I had to hold her, then push her, otherwise she never would have made it. Her look when we conquered that climb was enigmatic. It was a look of gratitude accompanied by a friendly squeeze of my hand, but was I wrong? Did I detect some other fleeting emotion?

At the top of the hill we all sat down gratefully. Even Walloomba seemed pleased to be able to sit and get his breath back. I noticed that he did not look forward however, but sat looking back at the way we had come as if expecting something to happen. After a while a small breeze sprang up. We all took deep breaths of it and Olivia asked Mrs Dujane what we were waiting for. She seemed agitated and said irritably that we were just to wait. We would see Art in due course. The breeze fell away and it became hot again. We moved into the shelter of some small gum trees where we displaced the birds that were roosting there. They flew off calling raucously and when they had gone there was complete silence for a moment. In that silence we all heard what I think Walloomba had been hearing for a while. It was the sound of someone moving towards us.

Olivia asked Mrs Dujane again why we were waiting. Mrs Dujane lifted a hand to indicate that we should all remain silent. Before anyone could speak a number of blacks joined us. They simply moved up the hill from the other side of it, women and children, including the little girl who had been Olivia's interpreter when we had left him to bargain for the boat. How on earth had they managed to keep ahead of us?

Mrs Dujane looked annoyed. She said something in a native tongue that made Walloomba answer shortly. He seemed put out too. Something odd was happening. Again we heard the noise behind us. As we did so we heard a small voice calling out from the other side of the valley or gully that dropped away beneath us. We all turned round, forgetting immediately whoever or whatever was arriving behind us. And there, on the cliff before us we saw a small white figure who yelled again and waved to us. Before we could anything some blacks emerged beside him and taking his arm led him away.

I was about to go with Olivia to where we had seen him, for surely this must be Art, when two men came over the edge where we had climbed up. One of them, short in stature and red-faced from the heat and temper demanded that he be given the papers straightaway. I looked for Mrs Dujane. I was not amazed to find that she had slipped away.

Chapter 8

It did not surprise me in the least when these men arrived demanding the papers. John Adam had agreed to help Olivia, and by sending me with her and Walloomba, had ensured that we got to Art successfully. He knew though that I would not be sufficient to get the papers back, so I was sure that he had arranged for other men to follow us and take them by force if necessary.

What was not clear to me was how Mrs Dujane, or Yellow Alice as she once was, had managed to lay hold of these vital documents. They were the ones that proved positively who legally had the ownership of the land. I had imagined that when the savages took Art they had the simple idea that they would just hold him until I, or someone with some sort of authority, arrived and gave them over in exchange for his safe release. I began to see that it was all much more complicated than that.

The plan that Mrs Dujane had hatched was to have the documents handed over by me once I had arrived. Everyone would assume that I had brought them with me. In this way she planned to spike my guns, making it impossible for me to say that I didn't have the papers or the authority to hand them over. I had to admit She had outwitted me, and I also had to admit that I admired her for it.

"Well, come on, give us the bloody papers", said red-face.

I knew that it was useless to pretend that I didn't know what he was talking about. My involvement in the past made it clear to me that I was in no position to deny any knowledge. I knew now very clearly what was at stake here; and it was not only the land but certain people's reputations and possibly their lives.

"I do not have them."

"Who does then?"

"Mrs Dujane has them."

"And where in God's Holy name is she?"

I drew Red-face to one side putting my face close to his, and trying to avoid breathing in too deeply. Red-face stank. Looking at Walloomba and Olivia, I lowered my voice.

"Ah! that's the problem. You see she has them until the black's dance when Mrs Gargery's son is to be reunited with us. She will then pass them to me so that I can hand them over in full view of everyone. It's a plan to make sure that there are too many witnesses for anyone to deny the truth later on."

Red-face spat, luckily missing my foot.

 "Truth, my ass! Do you take me for a fool?"

"Not at all. I assume that you are as sensible as anyone and that you want to get the documents on John Adam's behalf with the least effort and trouble to everyone. Is that not so?"

He growled something that took to be assent, so I hurried on.

I do not know where Mrs Dujane is at the moment. She has wisely hidden herself, and before you start thinking that you can threaten anyone, I have to tell you no one knows where she is at present. If you will only be patient I can assure you that she will return. Look, there are two of you and you are armed, so you only have to wait and your patience will bring its reward.

Most of this was guesswork on my behalf, but I was basing my guesses on what I knew so far, and the fact that Mrs Dujane had slipped away. I knew for certain that there was to be a corroboree. I was also fairly sure that she would be back. Red-face rubbed a calloused hand over his bristly jaw. I could see that my words were beginning to have an effect.

"Now, if just keep watching Mrs Gargery..."

"Oh! trust me, mate. Now that I have caught up with her I have no intention of letting her out of my sight."

He gestured to his mate who nodded as he told him what was happening. While he did so I went back to Walloomba and Olivia to explain that John had sent these men after us.

"What do they want?"

I answered Olivia's question as best as I could. As I did so I was frantically trying to think of a way to get us out of this mess.

In the meantime we sat and waited. Eventually Art appeared on the cliffs opposite us. When he raised his arms Olivia said:

"Thank God."

A gunshot rang out. Red-face swore as Art fell from the cliff. Olivia screamed. I pushed her back and scrambled forward over the side of a small ravine, where below I found a small black boy with patches of white clay on his body. He had been covered in white clay and that was why I had taken him for Art. Now, having come out of the pool, into which he had fallen, his white clay was coming off. He was completely unhurt, and he told me that the shot had startled him and that, as a result, he had gone into the pool below too soon. He had been meant to jump into it as part of a ceremony to mark his beginning to be man in the tribe. When the clay is all removed, the boy is left behind the man emerges and a new name is awarded.

Before he went he told me that Art had already jumped and was quite safe. I told Olivia this, having pulled myself back up to where she waited, and I also told her that Art would come back to us at the Corroboree. It was only then that I realised that the black boy had spoken in English to me. When I told Olivia that the boy had spoken English she said that he must have been Mrs Dujane's son.

It was the little girl, Nirwana, who had spoken to Olivia who was our real saviour. I sat beside her and asked quietly if she had any idea where Mrs Dujane might be. She turned her bright eyes on me and nodded. I asked her whether she could carry a message to her. Another nod. I spoke to her and she listened carefully.

"Are you sure that you understand what it is that I want you to do?"

She looked at me scornfully. No matter what their colour, scorn of stupid men is an inbuilt part of all female's minds! She slipped off so quietly that no one noticed her going.

Chapter 9

There were two things that I had to do. Each was important if we were to escape. The first was to find who had fired that shot, and the second was dependant upon the first. It began to get dark so we all moved back to the area where the corroboree was to take place. I sauntered off into the darkness and waited until my eyes were used to the limited light. Someone had fired that shot and I was pretty sure that it was another one of Red-face's party. I was sure that he was nearby and was keeping out of sight until he was wanted. I had borrowed Walloomba's knife and it was comforting weight in my pocket.

I waited until a small black figure joined me. She held out her hand and I put mine into it. I followed her, being as careful as I could be so as not to make any noise. Needless to say, as careful as I was, I was a blundering idiot compared with little Nirwana. We reached a spot where she let go of my hand sliding off into the darkness to wait for me.

I stood still. The black shape in front of me moved slightly allowing me to get a better idea of his size. A slight figure who would be wiry, I thought. He was so intent upon watching us at the corroboree that he had quite missed me coming onto him from behind. A lifetime of dealing with characters such as I expected this man to be, prepared me for anything that might develop when I tried to grapple with him. Nothing prepared me though for what happened next.

I put my left hand over his mouth to stop any possibility of him shouting. At the same time I put my arm around him whispering in his ear that if he moved I would push the knife that I held in my right hand up into his ribs and into his heart.

He didn't move. His hat fell off and a mass of hair tumbled down. I withdrew my hand slightly from his lips and was astonished when a feminine voice issued from them saying that if I would only let her go she would not struggle.

The woman that I now held was the person who had fired the shot. She explained to me that it had been an accident and that her role in this had been to watch while the other two men spoke to us. I took her gun. She sat down with a resigned air as I prised the bullets from the shells and collected a quantity of powder together in a kerchief. I tied it together in a little bundle and then I tied her hands behind her.

I told her that I was leaving someone to watch over her until we had got safely away; after that she would be freed. I then left her and returned to the where the fire was burning and the dancing was still going on.

Now all I had to do was wait until Art appeared. I told Olivia to point him out to me the moment that he emerged. I warned Walloomba to be ready to act. In time the newly made men appeared one by one. Olivia, sitting on the ground next to me alongside red-face and his pal stiffened.

"There he is."

I stood up, throwing the gunpowder in the kerchief into the fire making sure that I kept my eyes shut as it hit the flames and exploded with a great flash. It was easy job to grab Art then and drag him back through the wailing natives to where Walloomba was urging Olivia to run. As soon as she saw that we had collected Art she did so and all of us made off into the safety of the blackness that was outside the immediate vicinity of the fire.

Red-face and his companion were hampered by the blackfellas who charged about in a complete rout bringing both of them down.   By the time that they had disentangled themselves we were well away. It was Walloomba's turn now to act. We had to trust to his skills to get us further off to safety. Some shots were fired but they were at random and only made the natives roar more than before.

In a while we were well away and the noise of the upset natives died away. We rested. I caught Walloomba emptying his bag. He had collected several objects from the blacks and most of them he tipped out with a grunt. One of them, a beautiful carving of a snake he showed me. He told me that it was very powerful. It was certainly very attractive. He repacked everything, including the snake, and we continued with our escape.

Chapter 10

That night we found some deserted native shelters in a small clearing. Where Walloomba and I curled up to get some sleep. Art and Olivia were on the opposite side. I was dog tired and went to sleep the moment I laid down my head. It seemed to me that I had only been asleep for a minute when I woke to find that I was being attacked!

It was Walloomba who was hitting me. I could see him plainly in the strangest light. I thought that it could hardly be dawn yet. I had only just gone to sleep. To tell the truth, I was still half asleep. I was in that half awake state everything seems such an effort. I told Walloomba to stop hitting me. The light grew brighter. It was now a yellow colour. It began to turn red.

Now I knew what the light was, and the noise and smell that came with it confirmed what Walloomba was shouting at me. I tried to pick up whatever I could of what we had carried away. Walloomba stopped me saying that we must go. Animals were passing us as they tried to escape the flames. I could smell the hot bitterness of burned vegetation.

I ran across the clearing and pulled Olivia by one arm as I went. Behind me Walloomba caught Art and pushed him and me before him.

"Run. Run", he shouted.

The noise increased. I knew from its sound that we had very little time to save ourselves.

"Go down there", shouted Walloomba pointing to a split in the rock face.

Once we were inside we found that we had entered a deep gully at the bottom of which was a small muddy stream. We all crouched in the muddy water hearing the roar of the passing flames diminish as the bushfire swept on past us.

I could see that Olivia wanted to get out, but Walloomba made us stay. He said that we ought to remain there to let everything cool down. While we sat there in the mud, Olivia told us about the time that her Ma and Pa's shop in Sydney had burned down. She had gone to see it and remembered the smell. I could see that she was putting on as brave a face as she could, but even I was nervous.

We waited until the afternoon before we climbed out of our hole. There had been some rain so that made it easier for us. We went back to where we had been sleeping to see whether anything remained of what we had abandoned in our rush to save ourselves. There was nothing left, nothing at all, only ash. We stood and looked at what we had. It was precious little.

Walloomba opened his bag and showed me the stone snake.

"You see. We are protected."

I said nothing. He could cling to his superstitious beliefs if they gave him comfort. He saw my look.

"Why do you think we woke in time?" he asked.

I had no answer to that. Olivia overheard our conversation and seemed to think that we had a guardian angel. More superstition!

It was only later that I realised that I had lost one of my most prized possessions; it was the razor that my uncle had given me, made of steel that was so excellent that it took the finest edge when I stropped it. So far throughout our travels, I had tried to maintain some semblance of decency in my dress and general appearance. It was all very well for Olivia to dress like a native, but I thought that we white people should always make an effort. I began to see why they took that gong on the doomed expedition.

Each day I shaved my face and trimmed my moustache. I combed my hair. I am not a proud man, but I do own that there was a tinge of pride in me as I considered my fine head of hair, particularly as Walloomba's was a scrubby handful of white wool that would have looked better on a sheep's backside.

It was the fire that helped to save us, for when we came out of that great cleft where we had sheltered I realised that it had destroyed any trail that we might have left. It did give us a problem of finding our boat, but as it had veered away, carried by the wind in another direction our boat was where we had left it.

And, strange to tell it was full of water. The previous rains had filled it completely. Walloomba and I tipped it over, soaking Art and Olivia in the process. I was still afraid that we would be pursued that I made then what was to be a mistake. I collected together some poles, and using Walloomba's knife I trimmed them into more usable sizes.

My idea was that when we pushed our boat out into the stream we could allow the current to take us away from further trouble. I bargained on the fact that we could use the poles to keep us in the centre of the river and that would be enough to keep us away from snags and rocks. I didn't imagine that when we got further down the river it would narrow so much and shoot us through the rapids at such a speed that we would not be able to stop!

Chapter 11

With spray all around us, and deep cliffs on either side our little boat was driven through a deep gorge and into the sea. Our troubles didn't end there however. Where the swollen river met the sea was so turbulent, so full of swirling vortexes that we were nearly sucked under several times, and only frantic efforts with the poles enabled us to avoid disaster.

Mercifully we were able at last to bring our little craft round and it was driven onto the shore by the breakers. We had a welcoming party of savages that soon went off and brought us some food. It was Walloomba who persuaded them to do so. We stayed there for a while fishing and smoking what we caught for use later on. All the while I was wondering what on earth we could do to get us out of this fix.

Olivia seemed not to realise our true predicament. She told me that Silla and Kribdis had been overcome, so we were not to worry. She acted as if all our worries were at an end. I tried to act as if I had everything under control. I saw Olivia go along the beach and I resolved to follow her. I would go after her and in some quiet spot I would explain our true predicament, and I would also take the opportunity to tell her what I had been thinking and feeling.

I left Art and Walloomba to finish dealing with the fish. They were carefully smoking them, having partially dried them in the sun after using Walloomba's knife to gut them. I knew that I could safely leave them with this task. Art was enjoying being so helpful and the occasional word of praise from me made him glow with delight. Walloomba hardly ever said such a word. In his world, young men were expected to help and to become skilled. The reward for them was to participate in men's activities. Rather than praise, it was exclusion when you failed that was the spur to action. I set off and looking back I could see where I had left Art and Walloomba by the screaming flock of seabirds that were gorging on the fish guts that had been thrown into the sea.

I crunched my way along the beach only to pull myself up to a complete halt. In the distance I could see Olivia, but she had removed all her clothes and was standing looking into a rock pool. I felt a mixture of extreme attraction, which was tinged with a sexuality that I could not deny, along with shame at being so attracted. There was the woman that I had admired for years. I turned away. I could not violate her privacy. From the other side of the pool a flock of gaudy parrots flew up noisily. She turned to watch them and I used this diversion to draw back.

I told myself that there would be another opportunity to speak to her and when it came I would seize it. I felt that I had to unburden my thoughts to her. I was sure that I had read aright that she too shared at least some of those thoughts. Just as I had made this decision she came back, decently clad, and full of the news that she had found some wreckage.

Back we all went along the beach to see that what she had discovered was some old barrels. I immediately saw that this was exactly what we needed. We could shape some of the staves into a semblance of paddles and this would let us use our boat to go out to sea and to go south along the coast. What was more, some of the barrels were in such good condition that we could stow them in the boat to make us more buoyant.

Walloomba's knife was pressed into service once more, not only to carve the paddles, but also to help me lash a crude outrigger onto our boat. If we were to go to sea we had to be as seaworthy as possible. Walloomba made a simple sail. He explained that we did not need one that was too big, only large enough to move us along. Too big a sail would be unmanageable.

Olivia throughout this time lost her calmness and instead she swung from pleasure at the thought that we were like Robinson Crusoe, whoever he was, to despair when she saw how the breakers rolled in, breaking with a continuous roar on the sands. By contrast Art and Walloomba were steadfast in their support to me. I tried to cheer her up with stories about others who had made longer journeys.

Leaving the beach was actually comparatively easy. We were soon out to sea where Walloomba hauled up our little sail. And not a moment too soon, for on the beach came red-face and his mate. The fired at us but we were too far out by now for them to hit us. In any case there was a breeze, and we were a moving target. They must have come down the river by walking along the banks, not an easy task. And this had obviously held them up, for otherwise they would have been in time to catch us on the beach.

Not that it would have done them any good. Mrs Dujane had the papers still, and from what she had said to me, she intended to keep them. From believing that she really wanted to improve the lot of her brother and sister blacks, I had come to the point where I now believed that she was simply out to feather her own nest. Not that that worried me at all. Her life had been a hard one so in my opinion she was entitled to wrest something from it to make it easier.

I said as much to Olivia who took a most contrary opinion to mine, saying that in her view Mrs Dujane was not only hurting others by her selfish actions but was also an hypocrite. Seeing that she was determined to hold a contrary opinion to mine I stayed quiet for a while, then expressed my anxiety about being at sea at night.

This amused Walloomba who positively chortled with delight at what he saw as my ignorance. He averred that as long as we could see the moon and stars it would be possible for us to stay at sea. I was also uneasy at having to land. Again, he belittled me. He was sure that we would ride in safely through the breakers. I must say that the work that we had done on making our little craft more sea worthy was paying off. Art asked him about navigating, and Walloomba said:

" When the great serpent made day and night for us, do you think he would want to leave us all in darkness? The sun is there to keep us warm during the day. Night is for rest, but sometime we have to move at night, so stars have been put up to assist us. The sky moves round taking the stars with it.

"What about the moon", asked Art.

"Ah! The moon. How would men and women know about the passing of time without the moon."

He looked meaningfully at Olivia who blushed and said rapidly.

"Tell us more of your stories."

Walloomba did. He certainly enthralled Art who I could see seemed to believe that they were true. Olivia had something to say about that, but was taken aback when Walloomba reminded her that there were similar stories in the Bible!

Soon after this we had to land in order to cook food and collect water. Both Art and Walloomba had gone looking for a spring to replenish one of our barrels so I was alone with Olivia. This was the opportunity that I wanted. I wished to be clear with Olivia about my feelings. Her comments about hypocrisy sharpened my desire to say to her what had been on my mind for so long.

I thought that now I had shared so much with her that I knew what she thought and felt about me. I thought that by contrast with Pip, her husband, I was a much livelier specimen of manhood. I had gathered from her remarks, when she told me of her early years and her marriage, how disappointed at not being able to train as a nurse she had been. I was sure that she was just as disappointed with the life she now led. Why else had she gone with Mrs Dujane, if it had not been to seek another more interesting and fulfilling life. I could be a part of that life.

Given the chance I would have expressed these thoughts. But not only did Art and Walloomba come back in lively good humour at the exact moment that I was about to start, but they were especially animated, for on the horizon was a ship! My moment was gone. And not only was it gone but from the way that Olivia acted I knew that she did not wish me to say anything more.

It is often said that women have a sixth sense about the way men feel towards them, but I can assure you that men too can pick up the subtle hints that women convey in the tones that they use and the way that they stand and hold their heads. I knew. I knew.

Chapter 12

Leaving practically everything in our haste to put to sea, we pushed our boat through the breakers and paddled as quickly as we were able towards the ship. You can imagine my disappointed feelings as we did so. But soon other more serious matters concerned me. The ship simply ignored us and sailed on! I stood up. I shouted. I tore of my shirt and waved it frantically. I really believed that it was simply going to go on and we would be abandoned, when it slowly turned around and came back to where we sat slumped over and exhausted.

The ship stopped. We drifted slowly nearer. Crowds of men and women lined the side. At least one young woman had an opera glass that she trained upon us. The shirt that I had taken off to wave had fallen in the sea and had drifted away. Olivia held Art's hand tightly as she and he stood up when we bumped gently alongside a gangway that had been lowered. On it stood a naval officer in an immaculate white uniform with brass buttons that sparkled. He seized Art's hand and drew him up the gangway where some brightly dressed women surrounded him. Art turned, anxious to have Olivia join him. She, supported by a Grecian God disguised as another naval officer, reached him and left Walloomba and me without a backward glance.

I was left to make my own way up to the deck that felt hot to my feet that had been immersed in the water that slopped around our little boat. Walloomba behind me let out a cry. Men were pushing at the boat with boathooks.

"Stop!" I called out in a cracked voice.

The men looked confused. The Officer waved to them to continue.

"Stop that! Damn you. Let him on board."

I grabbed the boathook from one of the sailors and turned it on the officer. He backed away from me. He looked alarmed. I heard murmurs from behind me.

"Too much sun."

By now Walloomba had clambered up and pushed past a red-faced and scandalised sailor who went even redder as a black native walked on the deck that the sailor had scrubbed that morning. I took Walloomba's hand to lead him along to where I had seen Olivia go. The officer barred our way.

"Not him."

The sailors grinned. One laughed. Already our little boat was well astern as the ship was once more under way. Thinking that it would be impossible now for Walloomba to be returned to it I let go his hand. As I did so the sailor rushed at Walloomba and would have bundled him overboard had I not grasped the sailor's arm. I struck him so hard that his hat fell off. It tumbled along the deck slowly until a gust of wind caught it, and it would have gone into the sea had not a tall military gentleman caught it.

There was a gasp from the watchers. The sailor turned slowly having let go of Walloomba and was about to hit me back, when an even more resplendent figure came through the crowd.

Now everyone fell silent and the captain said to his officer and the sailors in as icy a tone as I have ever heard:

"Get back to your duties."

They departed. Now the officer was red-faced too. To me the captain said nothing. He also said nothing to Walloomba but indicated with a lordly sweep of his hand that he was to go below. I was only then that he spoke to me.

"My dear chap. Wherever did you find that fellow? Now, you look as if you need a bath and a shave. And, if I may say so, I do think that as a white man you might have made an effort at keeping up appearances. Excuse my not shaking you by the hand but you do smell rather. Come with me and my man will see to your needs."

The assembled watchers applauded, somewhat to the evident surprise of the captain who walked towards them making them fall apart like the red sea before Moses.

If I thought that I was now to be asked about who I was and why I was in such a predicament, I was mistaken. Going along the deck he went up a ladder ignoring me totally. His man drew me to one side and led me down another ladder to where I was treated to: a bath, very welcome, a loan of a razor, also welcome and change of clothes that were too large.

Now when I was allowed to regain the upper deck I was ushered into the captain's presence. He bowed to me and extending his hand, which was surprisingly calloused, he said, as he shook mine:

"Captain Percy Aveburry of the Ocean Star, at your service. I am so pleased to welcome you aboard now that I see you are indeed a Christian gentleman."

His raised hand forestalled my questions.

"Mrs Gargery is well and so is her son. As to that peculiar blackfella you had with you, he is messing with the stokers, who I might say in the course of their duties, which are keeping this craft in steam, are often almost as black as he is. So they ain't as particular as some of my crew, haha."

I thought that I should also laugh. After all we had all been saved, even that 'peculiar blackfella'. It was only later in a gilded stateroom where I marvelled at the silver and the crystal glasses as we sat at dinner that I was allowed to tell my story:

how I had been out prospecting and had been able to rescue Mrs Gargery and her son who had been exploring. I was upstaged in my efforts to do our story the justice that it deserved, by Olivia who described my noble efforts at rescuing her and her son from fire, flood and famine as positively quixotic!

She embroidered the simple facts in deference to the other ladies and gentlemen who shared out table all of whom wished to hear something exciting. Olivia obliged them. I realised that by doing this she was casting a cloud of trivia about the real reason that we were in the out back. I'm sure that we did not fool everyone. Colonel Sonspoor-Delany, the military gentleman who rescued the hat smiled knowingly at me.

As soon as I could decently excuse myself from dinner which was an excellent saddle of lamb with a superb cherry tart that I heard the steward say would fill us all up, I went looking for Walloomba. Sadly he was as drunk as I have ever seen him. The stokers whose hot work meant that they were also hot drinkers had given him a drink, and this had let to another and another. Now he lay on a bunk with his bag clasped to him. I begged the stokers to let him sleep it off and not to give him any more strong drink no matter what he said. Puzzled at my request, they nevertheless agreed to accede to it.

Leaving the lower decks I went in search of Olivia but found her surrounded by ladies all taking tea after their meal. I could see that I was not welcome so I returned to the gentlemen who were now onto the brandy and cigars, and very fine they were too.

Throughout the remainder of our time on that ship I never managed to get a quiet moment with Olivia. She had carefully covered our tracks and developed a story that she embroidered yet more when she sat with the ladies so I was not worried that our true reason for being in the bush would come out.

What I wanted principally was to be alone with her in order to tell her of my feelings and to see whether they were reciprocated in any small degree. A ship is a damnable place for privacy. Whenever I saw her, there were a bevy of ladies around her. The only place that I might have had a private word with her was in her cabin. As she shared this with Mrs Sonspoor-Delany, the Colonel's wife, this was impossible. In any case were I to be seen going into her cabin...

What a ridiculous situation! We had spent all that time together in the bush in such intimacy; now just to be alone with her was socially unthinkable according to the rules of decent behaviour. Finally I accepted the situation, but kept myself as much to myself as I could. I had been put in a cabin with a young man who offered me his bunk. Instead I slept upon a cot that the steward rustled up from somewhere. The young man seemed somewhat in awe of me so left me alone and I was grateful for that.

I made the occasional trip below to check on Walloomba. True to their word the stokers had refrained from giving him any sort of grog. The only fly in the ointment was the sailor that I had struck. On one of my trips below I was told that he was nursing a grievance against both me and 'that dirty black', and had said that he would get his revenge for having been humiliated. I pondered what to do.

In the end it all became quite simple. A collection had been made for we poor unfortunates by all the ladies and gentlemen, and it was pressed into my hand by Colonel Sonspoor-Delany whose quiet comment as he did so about myself and Olivia made my cheeks burn. Were my feelings for her so transparent?

Retaining my dignity I made a small speech of thanks that was received by smattering of gloved hand applause, then I withdrew. Going to the lower deck, I sought the sailor whose threats had worried me. He was extremely grateful that the lady and gentleman had seen fit to remember what small part he had played in our rescue, and assured me that the money that I had so generously given him would be used to drink our health.

Chapter 13

We tried to avoid the press. Our arrival though had somehow been passed on before us, so we had to answer some of their impertinent questions. One fellow hardly made any notes and I found out later that he had already written his story for the newspaper and had merely come along to make sure that there were indeed three of us. Later, when I read what he had written, I found that though he had made no mention of Walloomba; he had indeed reported that there were three white people rescued, but apart from that there was little else in his story that I recognised.

We took a cab, and as we got near to the shop I judged it best to be elsewhere when Olivia was reunited with her husband. So I said that I would join them later if that was suitable, for I was sure that once Olivia and Art were home she would wish me to explain to her husband what had happened to them. But my tact was wasted. For it was then that Olivia chose to raise again the matter of the book that she blamed me for losing. It exasperated me. I told her that she loved books more than people, and always would do so. I told the cabbie to drive away. She called after me, but I didn't hear what she said. I expect it was something derogatory.

I used the time to bathe once again and ensure that my moustache was looking its best then went to the Gargery shop. I arrived only to find that Olivia was still awaiting her husband. When he did arrive it was to tell a tale that amazed us as much as our adventures amazed him.

We ate a simple, but nourishing meal, prepared by Olivia's friend. Afterwards we all sat together feeling somewhat exhausted. I must own that it was pleasant to be able to sit together in this civilised fashion, but it was not so pleasant to be aware that I was harbouring feelings towards Phillip's wife that I would never ever be able to express. My unspoken thoughts were interrupted by Phillip.

"I am in no doubt that John Adam is behind all this."

I watched Olivia as Phillip made this statement. I felt sure that he was right. John had been involved in the business about the land, and I was sure that somehow he was behind what had happened to Phillip. The more I puzzled at this though, the more any sort of logical answer eluded me. Determined to get to the bottom of it, I rapped on the table to get their attention, slightly harder than I had intended. They both looked at me in surprise. I felt myself go red.

"Please forgive me. I merely wanted to say that you should be doing something about this, instead of merely discussing it. Before I leave you, maybe you should…make a decision about this?"

Even as I had hoped, Phillip picked up my more than broad hint and said that we all ought to go to see John. I demurred at being part of the group; after all, John Adam was my employer. I said as much, hoping that it sounded as if loyalty to John was my motive. In fact I was slightly alarmed as I did not wish to lose my position. Naturally I could get another, but John Adam's influence went very wide and I would need a reference.

I was stoutly overruled by both of them. Olivia, more vocal in her persuasion than Phillip, promised to stress how helpful I had been, so I had to concede defeat. And so it was agreed that the following day we would all 'beard the lion in his den' to quote young Art, who was then sent off to his bed, complaining that he would 'miss all the fun', for Livvy said firmly that he was to remain behind.

Chapter 14

Finally all three of us stood in John Adam's office. He had been told by Elaine Pomeroy that we had come to see him and he had given orders that we were to be shown in and that, after tea was brought, we were not to be disturbed. The tea came, brought by a nervous young woman who nearly dropped the tray. She managed to save it, and only a spoon clattered into the grate of the fireplace, that I knew from Elaine's gossip was a perfect copy of one in Balmoral castle in Scotland.

I picked up the spoon. John frowned in exasperation. He disliked bad service. He gestured for us all to sit. I wanted to stay standing despite the pain that I still felt. I could see that Pip would rather have stayed on his feet too. Eventually Olivia sat down, so we all followed her example. This was probably going to be a difficult session, with some hot words being exchanged, so we might as well be as comfortable as possible.

I looked at Phillip. He was the one who was most wronged by all that had happened. I thought therefore that I ought to let him start. I had forgotten however that although he might be simmering with anger, his actions, sometimes explosive ones, were more likely to be his reaction than words, so I spoke first.

"John, we are here because each of us has suffered as a result of something that we believe you started. I know something about the background to all this because, God help me, I have been employed by you. I was instrumental in assisting you to steal that land."

He raised a hand in protest. It was the word 'stealing' that upset him. His colour changed. I don't think anyone had had the temerity to speak to him in such bold terms for a long time, but I expect in his time in the goldfields he had been on the end of some accusations that were worse than being called a thief. I waited for him to speak.

"Don't let your tea go cold. My staff have gone to the trouble of making it; at least drink it while it is hot."

I might have known that he would counter anything that I said with a pleasantry. How often had he told me that: 'a soft answer turneth away wroth?' We were not to be diverted. We did sip our tea though. I returned to what I knew I had to say.

"So I knew that when you sent me with Olivia to rescue Art it was not as straightforward as it looked. When I discovered Mrs Dujane..."

He raised an eyebrow.

"Yellow Alice, John King's daughter. When I discovered that she was involved I knew that you wanted something more. I merely thought that all you wanted were the deeds so that your claim to the land could remain undisputed, and that you could continue to take coal out of the ground for the railways. I had no idea at all, not an inkling that your plans ran to more than that."

Olivia burst out:

"If it wasn't bad enough that Art was put in such danger, but you involved my husband too in your schemes."

She turned to Phillip who said to John, much more steadily than I thought he was capable of:

"Yes, and apart from Art, Livvy here was another one who suffered as a result of your schemes which I suppose make great deal of sense to you because they also make you a great deal of money. Come, Mr Adam, we have known each other a long time now. Be frank with us. I have a suspicion that none of us has the whole truth. I know some parts, and Jack here also has access to other parts. I have had some dealings with you in the past, dealings that make me think that, although you are interested in making money, you also have other interests. I have seen and heard you when you and Pip Pirrip were partners. I remember Estella..."

Philip's voice faltered to a stop at the look that John gave him when he said Estella. No one could have continued after such a look. It was sad one, it was grievously so.

At last John spoke. He spoke carefully and easily for some minutes and what he said completely floored us. We had come to attack him and to make him admit how badly we had been wronged. Now, after hearing him out, we were left feeling that it was we who were the guilty ones!

"When all this began it had to be kept secret. I can tell you now that it was a desperate policy to deal with a desperate situation. I know that you despise me as a money grubbing businessman. I admit that on that score I am a fit creature to receive your despite, yet I am also loyal to this country. I am a patriot."

Olivia whispered to me:

"Patriotism is the last refuge of a scoundrel. Dr Johnson."

John ignored her and went on:

"It may have been the scum of the old country that was sent here originally as transported felons like Abel Magwitch and your mother, Olivia, that began to raise it to its present height; but it was men like me and Pip Pirrip, and indeed you Phillip Gargery along with Olivia who have built upon the foundations that they laid. I cannot leave you out Jack, even though you could accuse me of pride in that I am proud of what I made you. Abel might have made a gentleman when he paid for Pip Pirrip's education; I made a geologist! And from what? What raw materials did I have to work with? No matter. What matters is that when they..."

"They?"

John waved away Jack's question.

"When they came to ask for my assistance to foil a plot that would not only destroy property and people, but would also destroy our new found country in the eyes of the world, of course I pledged my help; and in so doing I pledged yours too. News travels faster now. In the Russian war they had the telegraph and what was the consequence of news reaching England of the fiasco that the generals were passing off as running a war in the Crimea? I will tell you. The public became aware that they could no longer rely upon their betters because it was being revealed that they were no better. In fact they were a great deal worse.

So I was faced with having to go along with a conspiracy to counter a greater one that, had it succeeded, would have shown how we who were in charge in Australia were also lacking. We who considered ourselves better than those who we expected to obey our commands would be shown as no better.

John slumped back. His diatribe had been delivered at the expense of his health that we all knew was not as robust as it used to be. Olivia moved towards him and I could see that her compassion was about to destroy our opportunity to get at the whole truth. If John could play upon her sympathies she might draw Pip into that area of concern and I would be unable to get the situation under my control. I waved Olivia away. She flashed a glance at me that told me that while she would obey, I was losing her respect. As John had said 'no matter.' I spoke harshly asking John for more details.

"You can hardly expect us to accept your story if we do not know who was involved."

"I can tell you the names of some of the persons who were involved, not all, for that would betray confidences that I have sworn to keep. Possibly the most important is the

Governor of New South Wales, Sir Victor Albert George Child Villiers."

Phillip let out an exasperated sigh. I glared at him. John smiled.

"Two others you know Phillip: Alec O'Donnell and Con Fleaghly, but they are, or rather were, minor characters. To my mind though the main persons are all the members of the National Australasian Convention."

"Who the hell are they?"

Olivia looked reproachfully at Phillip's outburst. She said:

" I can tell you. It was in the newspapers.   I read about it. Let me see. There was a big conference at Melbourne at the beginning of last year. It was for all the Australian colonies and New Zealand. It was about getting together to form a..."

"federal constitution", finished John for her, then went on:

"Quite right. The intention is to get a union formed under the crown of Great Britain. It would strengthen ties between our countries so that if anyone attacked one of us the others would go to their defence. Of course it would also ensure more and better trade arrangements."

"Of course", I said.

John went on ignoring my ironic tone.

"All the politicians signed up to seeing what could be done. They decided that the way forward was to go away and persuade their respective governments to send delegates to a convention. It's that convention, called the National Australian Convention that was at risk."

Phillip said slowly:

"So that was what they were going to blow up."

John said:

"You can imagine how things would look if any members of the National Australasian Convention had been killed or injured in Sydney. All their efforts to find a way to bring about a federation would have crashed."

"But I thought that they were going to blow up the Royal Arcade", said Phillip.

"They told me that as it had so many shops and offices it was an ideal target."

"Yes, they wanted to start with an explosion there as a warning not to proceed with the Convention."

Phillip shook his head. I could see that he was not satisfied any more than I was. He wanted to know who these people were? Why were they so against a federation of like-minded countries. John would say no more. He said that he had already said too much, but just hinted at a particular nation that had caused so much trouble to England in the past.

Olivia looked at me. I looked away. I could go no further even though I thought Olivia would lose what little respect she might have for me if I kept silent. The trouble was I thought that I knew why her husband was implicated. If I spoke, she might hate me for saying such things as I thought I knew about her husband; if I kept silent she would dismiss me as a coward, more interested in my future employment than getting to the truth. She was not to be put off. Having found herself in the ranks of women who were demanding emancipation, she was scarcely likely to stop now.

"What I do not understand John is why it had to be my husband. Indeed why were we all involved?"

John sighed and looked at me. I tried to keep my face as impassive as possible, but I knew that my expression was betraying me.

There was a pause. I truly think that John hoped that we would all just go away. Then he spoke:

"Right. You want the full story. Here it is. When I knew that there was a conspiracy that might actually come to something, and that I was being asked to do something about it, I thought for a long time about just how I might foil the conspirators. I came to the conclusion that the only way was to get someone into their ranks who might be seen by them as being on their side. I'm afraid Olivia that it had to be Phillip, because of his past involvement with known thieves and his indiscreet remarks about that scoundrel who tried to shoot the prince that time. I thought that through one of my many contacts I could pass the word along on him and he would be recruited.

Olivia looked at Phillip. He met her look steadily, then spoke harshly to her.

"I thought that part of my life was all behind me. I admit that I helped the Kellys. Many others did. Once he was hanged I thought that that was the last of it. I said nothing to you about it. I came back and tried to lead a decent honest life. It seems that whatever I do I can't escape."

Olivia went to him and put an arm around him. She looked at John and merely said:

"Go on with your story."

"Right. Now let me say here and now that I never intended that Phillip would come to any harm. I thought that they would approach him and that once they had done so, I could let him know why I had manoeuvred him into such a position. He could then let me know exactly who was involved.

Then everything changed. Before I could get to him, he had come home only to find that you had gone off to look for Art. I know that I was instrumental in you going, but I made sure that you at least had someone alongside you to protect you. I wanted at the same time to get back those papers that Mrs Dujane stole from me.

Somehow the conspirators knew about you Olivia going off into the bush, and they used it to threaten you Phillip. Before I could get to you to explain what was happening you had gone back to them and I had lost my chance. Now I was at least able to keep track of you for when you did return to them I had you watched. Before this time I had no idea who I was dealing with. You had led me to them. Then just as they were about to be arrested in that house in the Rocks, you all disappeared.

You cannot imagine the relief that I felt when I heard that there had been an explosion outside the city and that you were there and that you were alive! What you didn't know was that the man you struggled with in the arcade was arrested as a potential thief. When you ran off he was so dazed that the men whose horse and buggy that you took held onto him until the police came.

When you told your story we immediately knew that we had no thief, but the instigator of all our trouble. So Phillip, I think that we can count you as a hero. We do have a problem though. For various reasons that I will not bore you with, the full story cannot be told. This means that I must ask you all to say nothing about this to anyone. And before you ask me, I have to tell you that the instigator has been allowed to leave the country. To have brought him to trial would have been a disaster as everything would have been revealed.

"Just a moment", Olivia said, "who were those people who came chasing after Jack, Walloomba and me? Jack says that one of them was a woman."

John smiled.

"In business there are always rivals. One of my biggest rivals, whose contacts in the Government are at least as good as mine, found out that I had sent you to get my papers. He arranged for you to be pursued. I cannot tell by whom. Probably some white men who have taken up with a black woman who knows the area. Possession is nine tenths of the law, you know; they simply thought they could take what was mine."

"Which you had already stolen from the rightful owners, the native tribe who lived on that land", said Olivia as she stood up to leave.

I said goodbye to both Phillip and Olivia when I visited the next day. I also tried to say goodbye to Art, but he seemed indifferent to my attempt at a farewell.

It was Art's behaviour that made me aware that my life was finished. I had not lost Olivia, for I never had her anyway. It was increasingly clear that she had no feelings for me, and indeed, never had had, any feelings for me. Of course that upset me. I could not but compare myself to her husband, that man whose dullness was such a virtue in her eyes that any bright liveliness on my part was seen as mere flashiness.

In all the time that we had been in the outback, and throughout all our trials it had been Art rather than Olivia who had grown to like me. I see it now. My occasional encouraging word to him was taken by him as a gesture of affection. He saw his father for what he was, is this not so with most boys? Girls I suppose are different. One sees them doting upon their fathers who are ever ready to spoil them. Olivia respected me

272

and my judgement but that was the full extent of how she saw things between us.

But, occupied as I became with my own thoughts and concerns I neglected when we were on the ship to pay attention to Art, who thought, as a consequence, that I had lost interest in him and his various activities. In effect, coming back to a father more than made up for losing my interest. I was no real loss to him. I was merely a surrogate, simply someone to fill in until his father became the father that Art always wanted.

And so I came to realise that there was really nothing left for me. I had been created by John Adam as his creature and I suppose I could carry on in that role. If I were to do so I would be simply part of the legacy of Abel Magwitch, whose transportation to New South Wales has gone on reverberating from year to year. I would be just an echo, not real at all. So I now realised that I could only be real if I was something or someone of importance in someone's life. Failing that I needed to create a new life for myself.

Epilogue

The Governor of New South Wales, Sir Victor Albert George Child Villiers, went back to England in 1893, declaring that the post could hardly be called serious nowadays, being chiefly of a social character. This was after he had hosted the Australasian National Convention in Sydney in 1891.

Later in 1897 the Australasian Federal Convention met and modified the draft that had been produced in 1891. Eventually an Australian Constitution was put into a Commonwealth of Australia Constitution Bill; it was given Royal Assent on 9 July 1900.

When John Adam died, his son, Federico, took over his father's business giving up his aspirations to be a painter.

Art became a qualified engineer, working on the Sydney Harbour Bridge, a structure that neither of his parents saw for they died well before its opening on March 19th 1932 by Premier Jack Lang, after six years of construction.

Phillip Gargery became employed by Edge & Edge, and in 1900 he assisted in converting to electric power the old steam tramway linking Brighton-le-Sands and Rockdale. Urged on by his wife he joined the Electrical Association of New South Wales.

Olivia Gargery was active in the rights for women movement for the remainder of her life. She was present at the celebrations when New South Wales' women were granted the right to vote in 1902.

Mrs Dujane disappeared, after selling the deeds to a piece of land that eventually became one of New South Wales' biggest coal mines. Her son, Teildo, disappeared too.

Walloomba left the ship that rescued him and the others soon after it arrived at Sydney. Then he was waylaid by the sailor who had objected to him coming onto his clean deck. Now he insisted on sharing his good fortune with Walloomba and got him drunk. That evening as they both staggered out of the drinking house Walloomba fell into the gutter where a cart ran over his legs. He died two days later of complications and pneumonia.

Lizbeth Wright persuaded her husband to adopt a daughter. When that daughter grew up she went to England where she worked in the House of Lord's library, marrying Lord Elthan of Birkgrade.

Elaine Pomeroy never stopped working for John Adam and one day, as she was recounting some gossip in the office, she collapsed and died.

Mrs Emilie Kaye became one hundred years old in 1944 and received a telegram from the King and Queen of England. She died two months later. Much later it was revealed that she had murdered her brother when she was a young girl in England.

Maybanke Wolstenholme Divorced her husband when the Divorce Amendment and Extension Act was passed in 1892.

Edward Jones continued drinking, became Town Crier for Perth, and died after a drunken fall from a bridge. Years later it came out that he was telling the truth about his exploits in Buckingham Palace, only slightly embroidered.

Jack King turned his back on geology and took up sculpture, becoming one of Australia's first well known artists. His "Great Serpent" carved in sandstone and coloured in the Aboriginal fashion caused a sensation when it was exhibited at the Paris Exposition of 1900. At the time that it was being exhibited, it was reported from Australia that a cave containing early aboriginal sculptures, including a serpent, suddenly collapsed having been completely destroyed by tree roots.

www.ingramcontent.com/pod-product-compliance
Lightning Source LLC
Chambersburg PA
CBHW060614030726
47498CB00005B/1672